HOLLIS

HOLLIS

a novel

JEFF GOMEZ

Harrow Books

© 2021 Jeff Gomez

This is a work of fiction. Names, characters, businesses, places, events, locales, and incidents are either the products of the author's imagination or used in a fictitious manner. Any resemblance to actual persons, living or dead, or actual events is purely coincidental.

For Darrell Zwerling

But now the remembering rushed down upon him as if it were a flood that had been damned and held back for too long while it gained a terrible force and momentum.

—JOHN WILLIAMS,
NOTHING BUT THE NIGHT

He dreams of water. A gigantic wall of water. An unstoppable force of massive blackness and death made of nothing but liquid. He tosses and turns in his bed as if caught in waves, arms and legs fighting uselessly against huge eddying swirls. When he's startled awake, finally free from the nightmare, it takes him a few seconds to register where he is, for him to notice that he's safe and on land. He finds himself panting and soaked with sweat. The large house is silent. His wife, by his side, barely notices. He's had this dream many times before; she's used to it. Grabbing his tortoiseshell glasses from the nightstand, he notices his hands are shaking. He gets out of bed, puts on his pair of slippers, grabs a blue pin-striped robe draped over a chromium armchair. As he exits the room and walks downstairs, he puts on the robe, tying the belt around his waist.

Needing air, he opens the French doors off the dining room and walks onto the veranda. It's a clear night and he can see stars and an almost-full moon. Cool air dries the sweat on his forehead, making him shiver. It's comfortable now, but earlier in the day it had been ninety degrees—unseasonably warm for late September in Los Angeles. The city has been baking in a heat wave that's lasted for weeks; the summer will just not end. There's also a drought. The rainy season should have started, but there hasn't been so much as a drizzle since last March. Southern California usually sees around twenty inches of rain, but this year there's been less than five. He can see, in the hills beyond his house, the yellowed grass and dry brush that look almost white in the moonlight. His own property, by contrast, is green and lush. This is possible because of the water that comes out of the pipes. Water he helped bring to the city.

Beyond the wrought iron table and chairs and a winding cobblestone walkway, a pond sits amid a patch of grass. He walks to the edge of the pond and kneels down, the lawn cool and wet against the silk of his robe. The pond, filled with salt water, is populated with sea creatures. Starfish, barnacles, coral, anemones. It's a miniature version of the tide pools he used to explore as a boy around the Monterey coast. He and his dad would walk around the beaches at low tide, looking for life in and among the craggy rocks and shallow seawater. When people would ask what they were looking for, peering down at the ground like that in their green rubber boots, the father and son would only smile instead of answer. They never even caught anything. Not once did they take so much as a shell or a rock home with them. They just wanted to look, to examine and be silent witness to the strange and amazing world where life began.

Even though he was fascinated by marine life and

dreamed of being a scientist, his father insisted he do something more practical. At Stanford he took an engineering course, found he had an aptitude for it, and decided he could do worse than make it his livelihood. A distant relative who knew someone at the water department in Los Angeles provided an introduction. After graduating early, he got the job and headed south. When his father died on his twentieth birthday, he was in the Santa Susana Pass helping to build the aqueduct that would bring water to LA. That was in 1912; it was his first week on the job. Back then he was just one of hundreds of men working on the colossal project. Twenty-five years later, he's now the man in charge. Chief engineer.

"Hollis, come back to bed."

He looks toward the house and sees his wife at the second-story window. Above her, the sky is already turning to purple. It will be morning soon.

"Yes, Evelyn."

1

STOP STEALING OUR WATER.

Hollis, seated at his desk, stares at the note. It's on thick white paper and has crease marks from where it had been folded into thirds. The words are scrawled in large block letters that take up the entire page. Russ Yelburton, the deputy chief, is on the opposite side of the desk. He cranes his head, trying to read the note upside down. Elwin Ransome, an engineer who works on the second floor, stands between both men. The large office is stuffy. It's barely ten, but it's already eighty-five degrees outside.

The building's air-conditioning strains against the heat, emitting a slow wheeze and only slightly cool air.

"I ran it up as soon as I saw it," says Elwin, slightly out of breath. A sheen of sweat is on his upper lip.

"Thank you, Elwin," Hollis says.

On the wall behind Hollis are his framed college degree and various awards and honors. One of them, a plaque featuring half a fire helmet painted gold, reads TO HOLLIS MULWRAY, A SMALL TOKEN OF THANKS FROM PASADENA'S FIREFIGHTERS. Along the back wall, a conference table sits perpendicular to Hollis's desk. Surrounding the table are four black leather chairs. Yelburton grabs one of the chairs, undoes a button on his suit jacket, and sits down. Both Mulwray and Yelburton wear light-gray suits. Elwin is wearing just slacks and a thin cotton shirt whose sleeves have been rolled above his elbows.

"Hollis, this is the third one you've received this month."

Yelburton speaks with the smooth easiness of an East Coast blue blood; he went to Exeter and then Yale before coming west. With his thin mustache and Brylcreemed brown hair, he resembles Ronald Colman. By contrast Hollis—thanks to his thin frame, penchant for bow ties, and salt-and-pepper hair and mustache—resembles a stiff Berkeley professor.

"Russ, it's nothing. They're just ... threats."

The inner door to the office opens and a secretary enters from where she sits in the foyer between Hollis's office and Russ's. Her pursed lips are painted dark red and her penciled-in black eyebrows are as thick as the letters in the note on the desk. Elwin is barely thirty, and both Yelburton and Mulwray are in their mid to late forties, but Hollis's secretary is pushing seventy. She's been with the department since it was founded.

"Mr. Mulwray, I called the police."

"Oramae," says Hollis, sighing, "I wish you wouldn't have done that. This is a departmental matter. We can handle it."

"But, Mr. Mulwray, I'm *frightened* for you. First the threats against the reservoirs, and now this."

"It's nothing we haven't seen before," Hollis says to the room. "There's a heat wave, a drought, and the bond issue's coming up soon for the new dam. It's bringing all kinds out of the woodwork."

"Well, I called them anyway. They're sending someone over." Before retreating, she instinctively straightens a slightly askew pen set that rests on Hollis's desk.

"Reservoirs?" says Elwin.

Hollis turns and can see, through the frosted glass of the inner door, his secretary pacing back and forth. He then faces his coworkers.

"I'm afraid it's not just the reservoirs. We've had people calling in threats along the entire span of the aqueduct."

"What kind of threats, Hollis?"

"The usual." He takes off his glasses and twirls them around. The movement causes a small breeze. "Dynamite. Bombs."

Elwin whistles.

It's happened before. The aqueduct has been attacked multiple times since it was completed in 1913. Over the years, saboteurs have managed to blow up small sections here and there, but never with any major or permanent damage. The water's never stopped flowing. And despite all the threats on the reservoirs over the years, there's never been an incident.

"Phone calls are one thing"—Yelburton points to the letter on Hollis's desk—"but what about that?"

Hollis opens a desk drawer and pulls out the two others. The paper and the writing are the same. One reads NO MORE STEALING OUR LAND and the other MORE PEOPLE ARE GOING TO DIE. The first two had been mailed directly to the office a few weeks ago, Hollis's name written on the envelopes in the same block letters. Both postmarks were from San Pedro. The one today Elwin found downstairs in a book of blueprints for the new dam.

"Where do you think they're coming from?"

Hollis shrugs and puts his glasses back on.

"What I want to know is how the one today got into the building." Yelburton turns to the young engineer. Ransome's only been with the department a few months. "Elwin, you didn't see anyone in the office who looked suspicious?"

He shakes his head and replies, "No, sir."

"Gentlemen, I'm sure it's nothing." Hollis gathers the notes and puts them in the envelope the first one came in. "Thank you again, Elwin. You can go back downstairs now. I'll let you know if we hear anything."

Ransome nods to both men and leaves, saying goodbye to the secretary on his way out.

Yelburton waits for the outer door to close before asking, "How much do we know about him?"

"Elwin? Seems like a good man."

"It just seems suspicious, doesn't it? Him finding the letter and running it up to you like that?"

"But he didn't find the other ones. And the writing isn't his." Hollis holds up the envelope. "I've seen his work."

Yelburton is about to say something else when the phone on Hollis's desk rings. He tosses down the envelope and picks up the heavy black receiver.

"Yes?"

"The detective is here, Mr. Mulwray."

"Already? Send him in."

After hanging up, Hollis stands and says to Yelburton, "The police."

"Do you want me to stay?"

"No, Russ. I can handle it."

Just as the secretary is showing in the detective, Yelburton leaves through a door that opens directly to the outside hallway. The detective is short and stocky and is wearing a cheap summer suit. There's an oval of sweat on the front of his light-brown hat. He and Hollis shake hands. The detective's hand is swollen and clammy.

"Hollis Mulwray, thank you for coming. Have a seat."

"Pleased to meet you." The detective produces a business card. "Wallace Holabird."

As they both sit down, the detective removes his hat and places it on the corner of the desk. Hollis examines the man's card.

"Wilshire Division. Been there long?"

"Five years. Am originally from Philadelphia. Doctor advised me to come out here for my health."

"I thought most people came to Hollywood to be in pictures."

"Not with my face." The detective smiles and pulls a pack of Camels from his breast pocket. "Do you mind?"

"No, go right ahead."

When the detective lights the cigarette with a Zippo, Hollis can smell the lighter fluid.

"I appreciate you coming on such short notice, Mr. Holabird. I just hope we're not wasting your time."

"I was in the area, so it was no trouble." He exhales a lungful of smoke. The smoke seems to raise the temperature in the room. "Your secretary tells me you've received some threats."

"Yes. Phone calls, mostly. A dozen or so to our main switchboard over the past month. And there have been these."

Hollis hands the detective the packet of letters.

"The first two were mailed. The latest one made it into the building somehow. It was found, just now, in an office on the second floor."

The detective slowly examines each letter. As he's carefully refolding the notes and putting them back into the envelope, he asks, "Any idea who might be sending them? Or why?"

Hollis sighs before answering.

"Los Angeles is a desert. We can't exist without water, but we don't have any natural resources of our own. When the aqueduct was built twenty-five years ago, the farmers in the Navarro valley weren't happy. Many felt we stole the land and, quite frankly, the complaints have never stopped. And then there's the matter of the Van der Lip Dam."

"Van der Lip?" The detective takes another puff and shakes his head. "I'm sorry, I'm not familiar."

Hollis sighs again.

"My predecessor, the first chief engineer—a man called Cross—was concerned about having enough water on hand for the city. The attacks on the aqueduct made him nervous, and various business leaders placed pressure on him."

"Business leaders," repeats the detective. "What was their stake in it?"

"With a reliable water supply, companies move here and build factories. This in turn creates the need for housing, stores, entertainment. Los Angeles can exist. Take away the water and we're just another town on the edge of a desert. So the department built a dam in Van der Lip Canyon fifty miles outside of the city. It was two hundred feet tall and held a year's worth of water. Twelve billion gallons."

As he stubs out his cigarette, the detective whistles. Hollis notices that he whistles better than Elwin.

"I don't see a problem."

"For two years, there *wasn't* a problem. But then the dam failed. All of that water rushed right down the canyon. Destroyed a power plant, swept away dozens of houses, tore up roads, leveled half of Santa Paula." Hollis looks toward the window. Above the building across the street, he can see mountains. Beyond those mountains is the canyon where it happened. "Five hundred people died."

"And you think some of the threats might be connected to that?"

Hollis turns back to the detective.

"My predecessor was put on trial for criminal negligence. He could have gone to jail for the rest of his life. But the jury—a panel of engineers, really—ruled that the failure of the dam was an accident. But people never forgave him. We had threats for years. They stopped for a while, but now"—Hollis gestures to the envelope on his desk—"it appears they're back."

The detective pulls another cigarette from the crumpled package. Before lighting it, he asks, "But why now?"

"Plans for a new dam have been drawn up, this time farther east, in Vallejo Canyon. I think all the news around the dam is bringing the old memories to the surface. The drought doesn't help, of course. Plus, construction on a scale like that would put lots of men to work. Hundreds. Maybe even thousands."

The detective leans forward.

"Is there any question the new dam won't be built?"

Hollis closes his eyes and hears the screams of women and children caught in the rushing water. He sees dead men tossed by waves. Hollis opens his eyes and looks at the detective.

"I'd be a fool to make the same mistake twice."

The detective places his cigarette in the ashtray and retrieves from his hip pocket a small tan notebook and black pencil. The line of smoke rising from the cigarette dances in the wake of the air conditioner.

"Do you mind if I ask a few general questions? It's just to get some background information."

"Not at all."

"How long have you been chief engineer?"

Hollis does the math in his head.

"Just about ten years."

"Can I have your phone number and home address? We may need to contact you there."

As Hollis answers, the phone in the foyer rings and his secretary answers it.

"Wife?" The detective looks up, his face shiny with sweat. "Kids?"

"Married, yes." Hollis pauses before answering the rest of the question. "And a child, yes. A daughter. Katherine. But she doesn't live with us."

"Katherine," Holabird repeats as he writes. "Is she grown? Out of the house?"

"Almost," Hollis says, forcing a smile. "She attends a boarding school in Mexico."

The detective writes this down.

"Do you feel that any of these threats have been directed towards you personally, or is this strictly about the policies of the water department?"

Hollis considers this. He's managed to keep a low profile over the years. His name is rarely in the papers, and most residents of Los Angeles don't even know who he is. His wife, however, is another matter. Evelyn goes to premieres, is a fixture of the city's social scene, has famous friends. She appears often in the gossip columns of Louella Parsons and Hedda Hopper. Hollis, more than ten years her senior, prefers to spend quiet evenings at home. Over the years there have been rumors of infidelity, but Hollis has never pursued them. Evelyn is Evelyn; he knows what he married.

"No, I don't—think they're personal."

The detective stops writing and looks up.

"Is there anything else you think might be important?"

"No, I think that's all there is."

The detective closes the book and puts it back in his pocket, along with the pencil.

"To be honest, Mr. Mulwray, there's not a lot to go on. If there's any escalation, or personal threats to you or your family, I can see about assigning a man to the building or maybe sending a squad car to your home. Otherwise, there's not much I can do. But be sure to let me know if anything else happens."

"I will, thank you."

Hollis walks him to the door that leads to the hallway.

"Nice to meet you, Mr. Mulwray. If anything comes up, anything at all, please give me a call."

They shake hands again.

"I'll do that."

Hollis shuts the door and walks back to his desk. He picks up the detective's card.

"Wallace Holabird."

After he sits down and leans the card against one of the pens in his pen set, he picks up the black receiver and presses the button for his secretary.

"Oramae, will you come in here for a moment?"

She appears a second later.

"Yes, Mr. Mulwray?"

"I'd like for you to get me the Van der Lip file."

"Didn't we turn over everything for the court case?"

"Sorry, not the departmental files. My personal file on the matter. It should be in one of the cabinets."

She nods, says, "Right away, Mr. Mulwray," and retreats back to her desk.

While he's waiting, Hollis hears noise from the street below. Spring Street is nothing but shouting and honking. The heat's driving everyone crazy.

The secretary returns with a dark-brown file folder stuffed with papers. After handing it over, she lingers.

"Is there something I can help you with, Oramae?"

"No, Mr. Mulwray." She begins to leave but stops and turns, motioning toward the file. "It's just—is this related to the detective? To the threats?"

"No, Oramae, this is something I've been thinking about for a long time."

"But, sir, I don't understand."

Hollis looks from the stack of papers to her.

"I can't build a new dam until I find out what happened to the last one."

She nods slightly and goes back to her desk.

Hollis begins to look through the file. It's a random assortment of things he collected in the days and weeks after the disaster. Trial transcripts, police reports, eyewitness accounts. The first few items are front pages from newspapers all over the country, banner headlines in huge type. DEATH FLOOD COMES IN DARKNESS. GREAT WALL OF WATER SWEEPS SLEEPING VICTIMS INTO ETERNITY. DEAD MAY NUMBER 400. He flips past these.

The next item is a photo from the trial. Noah Cross on the witness stand. His hands are joined and he looks down, face unshaven. At the time the dam failed, Cross was a giant. The success of the aqueduct had made him a legend in California and beyond. It had also made him rich. Cross, along with a small group of business leaders and politicians, had bought up land in and around the Navarro valley, land that was later sold to the city for a profit. But the Van der Lip disaster ruined overnight the public idea of Cross as a brilliant maverick who was able to literally move mountains. Held personally responsible, his name was in the paper for weeks. People put up signs in their yards that read HANG CROSS. As if that wasn't bad enough, his wife of twenty-three years was dying of cancer and would succumb just before Cross was exonerated.

It was around this time that Evelyn—Cross's daughter and only child—ran away to Mexico under mysterious circumstances. She returned a year later and, shortly after, Evelyn and Hollis began seeing each other. They were married the following spring. Cross wasn't invited to the wedding.

Putting aside the courtroom photo, Hollis finds another bundle of newspaper stories. In the days after the disaster, outlets all over the state competed for the tales of bravery and heroism that provided a welcome contrast to the tragic accounts of death and horror.

One story in the *San Francisco Chronicle* highlighted a group of telephone operators who spent hours at their switchboards notifying authorities about the approaching flood. They were said to have saved hundreds if not thousands of lives. The *Fillmore Herald* told the tale of a security guard who perished while waking workers camped out south of the dam. And the *Los Angeles Times* profiled a California Highway Patrol officer who had raced through the streets of Santa Paula blaring his siren and telling the sleeping townspeople to get to higher ground. He was later christened "the Paul Revere of the Van der Lip Dam." Hollis pulls out the story.

HERO SAVED DOZENS FROM A GRUESOME

DEATH. An accompanying photo shows the officer, Elmer Fowler, on the morning after the dam failed. He's being served a cup of coffee by a Red Cross volunteer while his motorcycle stands in the background covered in mud and silt. As Hollis skims the article, something catches his attention, a few lines in a paragraph toward the end.

> *Just before midnight, Fowler had stopped a car for speeding on the 99 freeway, just a few miles from Van der Lip Canyon. "I remember the guy was going like a bat out of hell. It took every inch of horsepower I had to catch him." The officer was just about to write the driver a ticket when the call came through on his radio. The dam had burst, and a massive wall of water was headed in his direction. Fowler let the driver go and raced to Santa Paula to warn the townspeople.*

The dam crumbled just before midnight, and most of those who perished went almost directly from sleep to death without knowing what hit them. There was no advance warning. But the driver mentioned in the story, the person who was racing away from Van der Lip *before* it came down—could he have somehow known? And if he did, why didn't he warn anybody else?

Hollis quickly searches through the file until he finds a

headline he'd flipped past a minute earlier. DYNAMITE THEORY NOW ADVANCED AS CAUSE OF BREAK. Even though the trial had acquitted the city and the department of any criminal wrongdoing, the real reason for the dam's failure was never officially decided. At the trial various engineers gave their individual explanations, but there wasn't any clear consensus. Some sort of foul play, including dynamite, had been mentioned but—without proof—investigations went nowhere. Sabotage was just another theory. After the trial ended, and the city set about working with lawyers and survivors on payments and settlements, people just wanted to put the disaster behind them. Life moved on. Noah Cross was removed as chief engineer and Hollis was given the job.

He picks up again the story about the CHP officer. After reading it a second time, Hollis picks up the phone.

"Oramae, will you get me Leslie Mayhew out at the California Highway Patrol? We should have his direct line."

"Yes, sir."

A few seconds later, he hears the familiar voice.

"Hollis, how in the hell are you?"

"Just trying to stay cool, Les. How about you?"

Hollis has known him ever since Mayhew was just an officer. Back then, Hollis was an assistant engineer. They were each just getting started in their careers; now they're both in charge.

Hollis clears his throat. "Listen, Les, I was wondering if you could help me. I know this is a shot in the dark, but I'm looking for an officer who was on duty the night the Van der Lip Dam failed. The name is Elmer Fowler."

There's silence for a few seconds.

"He was a hero that night," Hollis continues. "Rode through Santa Paula on his motorcycle warning the citizens. 'Paul Revere' they called him. Does that ring a bell?"

"Fowler, Fowler," Mayhew repeats. "God, yes! Boy, did all of that give ol' Elmer a swelled head."

"Any chance I could speak to him? Is he still located in Ventura or has he been transferred or—"

Laughter cuts Hollis off.

"Oh, no. He's not an officer anymore. Quit the department shortly after all of that. Last I heard, he was trying to make it in pictures."

"Oh, I—he's an actor now?"

Yet more laugher.

"Hell no, Mulwray. He's a goddamn *extra*."

"Oh, I see." Hollis twists the cord around his index finger. "Well, that *is* interesting, Les. Uh, do you think his old station would have a home phone number or—"

"I doubt it. Plus, Fowler's bound to have moved since then."

"Well," Hollis sighs, "thanks for the information. And be sure to give my regards to Doris."

"I will. And please tell Evelyn we'd like to have you both over soon."

Hollis hangs up, and even though it seems like a long shot, he figures he'd better try. He rings Oramae and asks her to connect him to Central Casting. After many rings, the phone is answered by a weary male voice.

"Yes, hello, I was wondering if you'd be able to give me some information about one of your employees. His name is Elmer Fowler. I'd like to get a home address and phone number."

"Employee?" The man almost chokes on the word. "Look, pal, we hire thousands of people for ten bucks a day to stand in the background. It ain't exactly General Electric down here."

"But I need—I'm looking for someone who works as an extra in pictures."

"Well then," the man chuckles, "I suggest you make a movie."

Hollis realizes he's getting nowhere. Looking down at his desk, he sees the detective's card. He clears his throat and tries again.

"Sir, my name is Wallace Holabird and I'm a detective from the Wilshire Division. I need to speak to Mr. Fowler *right away* as part of official LAPD business. Now, are you going to tell me where he is, or do I need to send a squad car down there to make you?"

"Geez, bud, why didn't you say you was a cop? Give me a sec, will ya?"

Hollis grins. While the man is getting the information, he hears more phones ring in the background. A minute later, the voice returns.

"Okay, it looks like we got Fowler assigned to a Shirley Temple picture out in Chatsworth. You got a pencil? I'll give you the address."

Hollis writes down the information, thanks the man for his help, and hangs up.

Chatsworth is a little town north of the valley, about an hour outside Los Angeles. There's not much there. Orchards, a few ranches, roadside diners. Hollis only knows about it because it's on the way to Van der Lip Canyon. Glancing at his watch, he figures he could grab an early lunch at Clifton's Cafeteria and be there by one. He might even go by the old dam after.

Hollis's Buick climbs the Cahuenga Pass on its way from Los Angeles to Burbank. Chatsworth lies another twenty-five miles past that. A hundred years ago, this land had been a site of war. Two battles were fought here between the settlers and the Mexicans. Construction crews sometimes still find cannonballs sunk in the dirt.

As he drives—the city blocks turning first to neighborhoods and then to farms—Hollis thinks about how he's going to gain entrance to the movie set. The detective's business card is in his suit jacket, but Hollis is nervous about pretending to be him again. It had been easy to fool the man on the phone. In person it would be far more difficult. Hollis doesn't look like a cop, and he knows it.

Thirty minutes later, he turns off the main highway and onto a dusty two-lane road. The flat landscape of orchards and ranches has given way to hills of dirt and rocks. Mountains rise high on either side of the road, the foothills pockmarked with huge boulders, oak trees, and sagebrush. The only other cars that pass are large trucks covered in dust.

After another couple of miles, Hollis turns onto a gravel road. Almost as soon as he does, he begins to see vehicles and equipment. Endless rows of trailers, huge trucks filled with lights and cranes, cars of all sizes parked in the dirt. Hollis pulls up alongside a catering truck, takes a deep breath, and turns off the engine. Getting out of the Buick, the heat hits him like a punch. It must be ten degrees hotter than it was in LA. As hot as Los Angeles can get, you'll occasionally get a cool ocean breeze. Out here in the valley, the air stands still.

Looking around, he sees dozens of people scurrying in all directions. Some are dressed in exotic costumes, while others—almost all of them men—are dressed in work clothes. Hollis follows a line of cables toward a crowd he can see up ahead. As he walks, he keeps a hand in his breast pocket. Fingering the detective's card, he's ready to pull it out if he's stopped and questioned. But nobody stops him. He passes a huge field set up with tables and chairs. Men in white hats and jackets are putting out plates, glasses, pitchers of water. Everyone seems to have a job to do, and no one pays Hollis any attention.

After fifty yards, he stops. The workers suddenly form a perimeter around a small clearing. Just beyond the expanse of sandy ground there's a set of stone steps leading up a hill. At the top of the hill an ornate gate between two stone towers sits on flat outcroppings of blond rock. Men with dark skin, dressed in long robes and turbans, stand along a low wall built between the two towers. Long rifles lean against the wall as the men smoke.

Hollis can also see a number of lights, a camera, and a series of barstools and chairs. Under an umbrella—the only shade in the area—two men confer and point to various points on the steps and up toward the towers. Everyone else just stands around.

Hollis turns to a young man wearing a linen shirt and beige pants. In the young man's hand is what appears to be a small blackboard. On the front are some words and numbers in white chalk. All Hollis can see is the name J. FORD.

"Excuse me, but I'm looking for Elmer Fowler. He's an extra, I believe. Central Casting told me he was working here this week."

The young man looks over. Hollis is the only person wearing a suit, so the young man figures he's from the studio. This might even be the producer.

"Try over there, sir." He points toward where a group of men are standing. They're also wearing turbans and robes, except their robes are dirty and threadbare. Beyond them, a man in a cowboy hat wrangles a pair of black horses.

"Thank you."

Hollis approaches the small group.

"Excuse me," he says to the first man he comes to, "I'm looking for Elmer Fowler."

The man has a mustache and a long beard, except Hollis can see that both are fake. His face has also been artificially darkened. The man just shakes his head and walks away. Hollis tries a few more from the group until one finally responds. The man turns and says to a tall figure at the far edge of the group, "Hey, Elmer, this guy's looking for you."

A man, dressed like the others, steps forward.

"Elmer Fowler?"

"Yeah, that's me." He squints at Hollis. "Who wants to know?"

Despite the costume, Hollis can tell that it's the same man he saw in the newspaper clipping that morning.

"My name is Hollis Mulwray. I'm with the water department."

Fowler laughs.

"What, you came all the way out here to tell me I forgot to pay this month's bill?"

"It's nothing like that." Hollis nervously adjusts his glasses. "I want to ask you about the Van der Lip Dam."

Fowler looks down at the ground and kicks at the dirt. "I'm all done talking about that, mister. You go find yourself some other chump."

"Please, it's important."

Fowler looks up.

"How important?"

Hollis pulls a five-dollar bill from his wallet. Fowler's eyes light up. He takes the money and follows Hollis as he walks a few yards away from the group.

"The night the dam failed, *before* it failed, you stopped a car for speeding. It was driving away from the dam."

Fowler shrugs, causing his turban to fall to one side.

"Do you remember anything about that?" Hollis continues. "What kind of car it was? What the man looked like?"

"Look, buddy, what's this all about? That was a long time ago and I—"

"Please, try and remember. It's important."

Fowler finally considers the question. "Before it failed," he repeats. "Sure, I remember. I got the call about the dam just as I walked back to my motorcycle to get my ticket pad. Boy, was the driver relieved."

"Relieved, why? Because of the ticket or because of something else?"

"What do you mean? What else could it have been?"

"Well, do you think he might have heard your radio? Did he know the dam had failed?"

Fowler shakes his head.

"No, I'd parked my bike ten yards behind the car. You have to remember, this was out in the middle of nowhere. It was practically midnight. You meet some crazies and I was all alone—my partner had called in sick. I wasn't about to take a slug to the chest if I didn't have to."

"When you told the man he could go, didn't he ask why?"

Fowler, in trying to remember, puts his hand to his chin. The makeup comes off on his fingers.

"I didn't give a reason and he didn't ask. He just took off, peeling out. In just a few seconds he was going as fast as he'd been when I pulled him over. Made me want to catch him and write the ticket after all, the bastard."

"Do you remember anything else?"

"Nothing more than I've already told you. Believe me, I remember an awful lot about that night—stuff I wish I could forget—but not him."

"Please," Hollis begs. "There must be something else."

While Fowler's thinking, a man in a cloth cap shouts out, "Places, everybody! Places! We're going to shoot another one."

Hollis gets nervous, thinking he's going to lose Fowler. But Fowler just stands there, still trying to remember. None of the men from his group make a move; this must not be their scene. The animal wrangler from before walks the two horses up the steps, while another man in a cowboy hat appears and guides a pair of camels to the foot of the stairs. The camels are carrying white bundles on their backs. Other workers appear and tend to the scene, placing rocks here and there and adjusting the costumes of the men who enter the scene and take the reins of the animals.

"I remember something," Fowler finally says, "although I don't know what it means."

"Yes?" Hollis turns back to the man. "What is it?"

"The driver said a name. Essie. I mean, I'm sure he said *more* than that, but that's all I can remember."

"Essie? Are you sure?"

Fowler nods.

"Essie," Hollis repeats. The name doesn't mean anything to him.

"Maybe that was his excuse," Fowler says. "You know, a sick wife or a kid or something. Essie may have been his daughter. Believe me, I used to hear all kinds of stories."

In front of them, the workers retreat from the scene, leaving only the animals and the men in costume. Up on the wall, on either side of the gate, the men have put out their cigarettes and are now holding the long rifles and staring down the steps menacingly.

After examining a few more details, the man in the cloth cap says to the figures in the shade, "Okay, Mr. Ford, I think we're ready."

After receiving a faint nod, the man in the cloth cap yells, "Roll camera!"

A man behind the camera answers back, "Camera's speeding."

The man in the cloth cap yells, "Slate!"

The young man Hollis saw before with the blackboard runs in front of the camera. The top of the blackboard is hinged. He raises it and then brings it down fast, causing a loud clap. He shouts, "*Wee Willie Winkie*, twelve apple, take four," and then runs out of the shot.

After giving the scene a final look, the man in the cloth cap yells, "Action!"

The animals and the men trudge up the steps and toward the gate. After they've walked a few yards, the man in the cloth cap yells "Cut!" Everyone stops and looks toward the umbrella. A man steps forward and places his hands on his hips.

"That's the director," Fowler says, nodding with his chin. "He's worked with lots of big names. Edward G.

Robinson, Will Rogers, Boris Karloff, even Wallace Beery. You like wrestling pictures?"

Hollis shakes his head.

"Anyway, I spoke to him yesterday. Said he'd put me in his next picture, and *not* just in the background."

Hollis looks around. All he sees are men in turbans and some animals. At the far edge of the clearing there's a huge trailer that looks expensive. The door says S. TEMPLE. He asks, "What's this movie about, anyway?"

"All I was told is this is supposed to be India. Most everyone"—he waves his arms over the scene—"is supposed to be Indian. Except for the ones who don't have the shoe polish on their faces—*they're* supposed to be British."

The man in the cloth cap confers with the director. There's a lot of headshaking. Finally, the man in the cloth cap announces, "Okay, everyone, that's lunch!"

The animal wranglers run to retrieve the horses and camels, while the rest of the cast and crew begin to walk back toward where Hollis saw all those tables and chairs.

As the men under the umbrella continue to discuss something, the door to the trailer opens and a small girl steps out. She's wearing a tartan kilt and a military jacket. Her blonde curls bounce underneath a pith helmet as she walks. Hollis has only ever seen her in photographs. As she passes, three adults follow behind, their heads bowed. Everybody remains quiet. Nobody moves.

"Just look at her," whispers Fowler, "nine years old and she's got the whole fucking world on a plate. That just don't seem fair."

The group of extras begins to follow the rest of the crew. As one of them waves for Fowler to join them, he turns to Hollis.

"You want to stay for lunch? We got a hundred people here—I doubt they'd notice one more."

Hollis looks at his watch.

"No, but thank you, Elmer, for the information. I appreciate it. And listen, if you think of anything else, will you let me know?"

Fowler hesitates before nodding his head yes.

Hollis reaches into his various pockets looking for a business card, only to discover he forgot to bring any. The only spare piece of paper he has is the detective's card. On the back he writes his name and phone number. When he hands it to Fowler, the man's eyebrows shoot up.

"You sure you're not in some kind of trouble, Mr. Mulwray?" He waves the card. "Those LAPD boys play for keeps. Believe me, I know."

"It's nothing like that, I assure you."

Fowler just nods, lifts up his robe so he can put the card in his trouser pocket, and then jogs to join the other extras as they make their way toward lunch.

Hollis, as he walks slowly back to his Buick, repeats the name under his breath. "Essie. Essie. Essie."

It's a twenty-minute drive to Van der Lip Canyon from the movie set in Chatsworth. All the roads leading up to the dam were destroyed in the flood, so Hollis has to park and walk the last mile. A path of hard-packed dirt once ran around the back of the dam, but that was demolished months after the disaster to discourage people from visiting the site. A large chunk of concrete from the center of the dam had somehow remained standing, and it became a draw for people, nicknamed "the Tombstone." Dozens drove out every weekend to take pictures and touch with their own hands where the tragedy had begun. When a young man playing on the structure fell to his death, the decision was made to bulldoze the whole area.

As Hollis walks on the rough and uneven ground, pebbles and sand seep into his shoes. Pausing, he takes off his hat and wipes down his forehead with a handkerchief. He knows this is madness, coming all the way out here, but he has to see it again for himself. He has to try and solve the mystery.

Hollis stops when he's about twenty yards from where the face of the dam used to be. Finding shade from a cottonwood tree high up on the canyon wall, he sits down on the dry riverbank. He stares at the big open space, the gap that was once filled.

He and Noah Cross inspected the dam the day that it failed. The dam keeper, a German named Bischopfer who lived at the dam with his young son and girlfriend, had reported a leak that morning. Muddy water was seeping through a crack on the east side. Even though Cross was sure it was nothing—cracks often appeared in dams; it was just a sign the concrete was settling—he and Hollis paid a visit. They met with Bischopfer and examined the leak. It only took Cross a minute or two to declare that everything was fine. They returned to Los Angeles in Cross's plush Marmon sedan, driven by his chauffeur. They were back in their offices by lunch. The dam burst that night. A year's worth of water shot down the canyon, sweeping clean everything in its path. Telephone poles snapped, oil derricks crumbled, trees were stripped of their leaves. The dam keeper's body was never recovered. His son and girlfriend were found miles away, under four feet of sludge.

Hollis was at home working when it happened. He was about to make a note on a set of blueprints when the lights went out. Most people in Los Angeles wouldn't have thought anything of it—losing power was a minor inconvenience that happened from time to time—but Hollis knew where the city's electricity came from. Harnessing water in California also meant producing electricity, and a huge power station had been built just south of Van der Lip. A whole community had sprung up around it. People lived there with spouses and kids; sixty-seven people called it their home. Only three survived the night. When his lights went out, Hollis's mind instantly flashed back to that morning, to the dam, to the leak. He was grabbing for his coat before the phone even rang.

The next few days passed by in a fog. In towns all along the flood's path, authorities rescued who they could and collected the bodies of those who had perished. Any empty space was transformed into a makeshift morgue: pool halls, church basements, theaters. The dead were everywhere.

The quest for answers started immediately. Engineers, geologists, and academics were brought in to look at the plans for the dam. Every inch was inspected, trying to find the error. Journalists also descended and began asking questions. Rumors ran rampant. Some said the dam was brought down by disgruntled farmers. Others insisted it was an inside job. One newspaper reported it was the work of anarchists. Another blamed socialists. There had been all kinds of bombings around Los Angeles, including the destruction of the Times building in 1910. The idea of foul play was widespread and widely believed.

Hollis did his best to consider every argument, explore every conspiracy. Cross, incapacitated with grief over the deaths and by his wife's battle with cancer, was of no help.

The reports that finally came back as part of the various official investigations hinted at all kinds of engineering reasons for why the dam failed—there was an insufficient base width, no allowance was made in the design for uplift or earthquake stresses, the dam contained no inspection galleries and no contraction joints—but none were deemed conclusive. Everything was just a theory. Hollis wanted the truth.

The trial took six weeks. As the verdict was read, the room was silent, the tension palpable. "We, the jury, find no evidence of criminal act or intent on the part of the Bureau of Water Works and Supply of the City of Los Angeles, or any engineer or employee in the construction or operation of the Van der Lip Dam, and we recommend that there be no criminal prosecution of any of the above by the district attorney." Noah Cross was shaken but declared innocent. The dam's failure was just a horrible accident, an act of God. This gave most people the closure they were looking for. That wasn't good enough for Hollis.

For a year he pored over the plans, trying to spot anything important that he might have missed. He reread the geological surveys, went over the court transcripts, made trips out to the site. He stayed awake countless nights looking for answers. On the evenings he managed to sleep, his dreams were haunted by giant black worlds of water—nightmares that recently returned. And even though he finally had to accept defeat and move on, it was always there in the back on his mind. The question he was never able to answer. What happened that night?

Hollis thinks about the man Elmer Fowler stopped the night the dam failed. Could he be connected somehow? Was he rushing away from the disaster because he'd just played some role in causing it, or was it just a coincidence? In the days after the tragedy, boxes of dynamite were found near the site. More boxes were found in a warehouse nearby. Neither could ever be conclusively connected to the dam.

There were also reports of dead fish found in shallow ponds downriver from the dam. It appeared they'd been killed by a powerful explosion. It was yet another sign that pointed to sabotage. However, any attempts to tie this to the official explanation went nowhere.

Hollis thinks of the recent threats, the notes and phone calls. Before the Van der Lip failed, they'd received similar warnings. Was one of them true, or did some crank somewhere just get lucky? After all, in the ensuing decades—as he told the detective—threats have continued to come in without any sort of major attack or incident. In the past, threats had always just been that. They didn't mean anything. Now he's not so sure.

Looking up, Hollis sees a huge hawk fly low over the canyon. It glides around and around in wide circles before coming to rest on an old wooden sign nestled among a group of sycamore trees. He gets up and approaches the bird, wiping sand from his hands on the seat of his thin wool pants as he walks. When he's a few feet away, the hawk launches itself into the air.

Now that he's closer, Hollis can see pale words painted onto the bleached and cracked sign. RESERVE STORAGE FOR THE CITY OF LA. Squinting, he can see more, but the words are covered by sagebrush. Hollis approaches and pushes down the shrubs, dried leaves cutting his hands. He stands back, breathing heavily. The words are faint and faded, and only half are readable.

DEDICATED 19
NOAH H. CROSS, CHIEF EN
SAM J. BAGBY, MAYOR OF L

Before the dam ended all those lives, it ruined Cross's and Bagby's relationship. The initial plans called for the dam to be located southwest of Van der Lip Canyon, on a huge tract of land owned by Bagby. He and Cross had a handshake deal but, when it came time to sign the papers, Bagby tripled the price. Cross pulled out of the deal, and a new location for the dam was hastily found. The incident caused a rupture in their friendship; when it finally came time to dedicate the dam, Bagby—even though, as mayor of Los Angeles, he'd pushed for the dam for years—didn't attend the ceremony.

Hollis wipes down his forehead with a handkerchief and heads to the Buick.

By the time Hollis makes it back to Los Angeles, the heat from earlier has subsided and a cool breeze enters his car from the open windows. The sky is pink and streaked with cottony clouds. As the city slowly comes into view, Hollis decides to drive home rather than return to the office.

As he pulls up to the house, he sees Evelyn's cream-colored Packard gleaming in the driveway. Just beyond, the gardener is pulling weeds from under a row of bougainvillea. He turns at the sound of Hollis's Buick and bows repeatedly. Hollis parks, gives a wave, and enters his home.

Inside, he can smell dinner being prepared. Passing the dining room, Hollis sees two Mexican maids setting the table. He finds Evelyn in the library talking to the butler. They turn as he enters the room.

"Darling," she says, "you're home early. Is everything okay?"

Hollis takes off his hat, hands it to the butler, and bends down to give his wife a kiss on the cheek. Her hair is marcelled, and her lips are painted in a red Cupid's bow. Her eyebrows are thin pencil marks, and she's wearing a green-and-red peplum dress with plastic musical notes for buttons. She must have met friends for lunch at the California or Jonathan Club.

"Everything's fine, dear." He sits down in a brown leather chair. When he does, a cloud of dust flies up from his clothes.

"Sweetheart, your shoes. Those trousers." She points. "You're a mess."

Hollis looks down. His shoes are covered in dirt and the cuffs of his pants are filthy.

"I'm sorry," he says. "I forgot."

"What happened? Where were you?"

Before explaining, he turns to the butler.

"Kahn, could you get me a cocktail?"

The butler bows and says, "Old-fashioned?"

Hollis nods.

"And for you, Mrs. Mulwray? Tom Collins with lime, not lemon?"

Keeping her eyes on Hollis, she answers, "Yes, thank you."

After the butler leaves the room, Hollis lets out a long sigh.

"I went to Van der Lip today."

Evelyn sits up.

"But why, darling?"

"It's this new project, the dam in Vallejo Canyon."

"What about it?"

Hollis takes off his glasses to clean them.

"I can't go through with it until I find out what happened at Van der Lip."

"But I thought all of that was settled. The trial, my f-father..."

Hollis puts his glasses back on.

"I know what all the reports said. I've never believed them."

She turns and grabs a pack of Lucky Strikes from an end table. The green-and-red packaging matches her dress. She lights the cigarette with an ornate glass lighter in the shape of a monkey.

"Well, then what do you think happened?"

"Sabotage, maybe. Dynamite."

The butler returns with the drinks on a silver tray. After Hollis and Evelyn retrieve their cocktails, Kahn nods at the dirty shoes.

"Pardon me, Mr. Mulwray, but would you like me to get your slippers?"

Hollis gives a quick chuckle and replies, "Yes, Kahn, thank you."

When Hollis lifts the drink to his lips, his wife notices the cuts on his fingers.

"And your hands, darling." She points again.

Hollis looks at them and shrugs.

"I was ... looking for clues."

Evelyn puts her cigarette in an ashtray and leaves the room. Hollis takes a long sip, sinking further into the chair. Evelyn returns with a bottle of hydrogen peroxide and some cotton balls. She sits on a velvet ottoman and dabs at the wounds.

"My husband," she says wryly, "the private detective."

The butler reenters the room with the slippers. He places them beside the chair.

"Thank you, Kahn."

Evelyn returns to her own chair and retrieves the lit cigarette.

"It's probably nothing," Hollis says, trading his dirty shoes for the clean slippers. "But I had to go and look."

Evelyn finishes the cigarette and starts another.

"Well, promise me you'll be careful."

He picks up a copy of *Southwest Review* from a glass coffee table.

"I will, dear," Hollis answers. "How was your day?"

"It was fine. I met Violet at Perino's for lunch. She's going up to San Francisco on the 9:45 train. Should be up there most of the month. Asked *me* to drop by every few days to water her plants."

Hollis looks over.

"All the way out in Santa Monica? Don't they have a gardener?"

Evelyn drains her glass and laughs.

"Yes, but he only comes once a week and she doesn't trust him. Says he steals from her, although I can't begin to think what there could be that a *gardener* could steal."

This makes him think of his mother. She's in a rest home located between Malibu and Santa Monica.

"That reminds me. Maybe I'll stop in and see Mama soon."

Evelyn says, "If you do, please tell her I said hello."

His mother never liked Evelyn, never approved of her past.

"She'd like that," he lies.

The butler appears yet again in the doorway.

"Dinner is served."

2

Hollis's desk is covered in files. Hundreds are stacked into huge, teetering piles. An empty box marked PERSONNEL sits on the floor. He's spent all morning searching for the name Elmer Fowler gave him the day before. The records go all the way back to the 1870s, when the company consisted of a handful of men whose sole responsibility was to remove rocks and debris from ditches. They were called *zanjeros*, and it's where Noah Cross got his start. Nowhere in any of the folders does he find any mention of an "Essie."

Hollis picks up his phone.

"Oramae, could you come in here, please?"

She appears a second later.

"Yes, Mr. Mulwray?"

"Could you get me the department's payroll files?"

"Going back how far?"

"Starting in 1920, please."

She lets out a huff.

"Mr. Mulwray, I *wish* you'd tell me what this is regarding."

"Please, Oramae. The files."

She reluctantly nods. As she's leaving the office, Russ Yelburton enters. He throws a report onto Hollis's desk. It lands on top of a stack of files.

"We just received the independent assessment of the Alto Vallejo plans."

In the wake of the Van der Lip disaster, a law was passed that all large municipal projects had to be appraised by an outside council of experts. No longer would one man be able to make decisions that affect thousands of people.

Hollis picks up the folder.

"What does it say?"

"The dam, the plans—they're sound."

Hollis tosses the document back to his desk and shakes his head.

"You can't put it off forever, Hollis. The bond issue is

coming up. The city council hearing is next week. And look, Bagby has an editorial in today's *Times*."

As Russ hands him a folded newspaper, Hollis glances at the headline: "The City Must Have Water." Sam Bagby, the ex-mayor, is one of the biggest proponents for the new dam. In the years since he left office, he's become an adept businessman, making millions in real estate.

"I realize all of that, Russ. But while I'm chief engineer, they'll do what I say."

Russ takes back the newspaper and the report, placing both of them under his left arm. As Hollis begins to gather and stack all the folders, in order to make space for the payroll files, Yelburton asks, "Hollis, what's all this?"

"Nothing, Russ. Just trying to sort out a personnel matter."

"This isn't about Elwin, is it?"

Hollis looks at him.

Yelburton continues, "The note from yesterday?"

Hollis looks back to the folders.

"No, it's nothing like that."

"That reminds me, how did it go with the detective yesterday?"

"About like I expected. Said he couldn't do much if all we've received are threats. Oramae really shouldn't have called him."

Russ considers this.

"Maybe we should get some help of our own."

Finished with the stacking, Hollis sits back.

"What do you mean?"

"Well, if the police can't help until something actually happens—which, by then, it will be too late—maybe we should get some men of our own."

"Who?"

"There are people. Private firms, ex-policemen, investigators. You'd be surprised."

"I don't know, I'd hate to have a bunch of two-bit Pinkertons patrolling our sites like they're hotel detectives. It'll give the public the wrong opinion."

"I'm sure they'll be discreet." Yelburton smiles his best smile. "Let me handle it."

Hollis is nodding as the secretary enters with an arm full of large brown folders. Russ leaves as she places them on Hollis's desk. It's a mountain of paper.

"Thank you, Oramae." He glances at the grandfather clock on the far wall. It's almost noon. "One more thing, could you order me a sandwich?"

"Yes, Mr. Mulwray."

She leaves, closing the door behind her.

Hollis digs into the new batch of documents. After a half hour of looking there's no mention of an *Essie* but, amid the pay stubs and tax forms, he finds something interesting. A memo about a trio of workers. It seems three men at the Van der Lip Dam quit on the same day, with no advance notice. They just reported to the foreman that they'd had enough and walked off the job. This kind of thing happened often in the field, where conditions were grueling; prior to the dam failing, plenty of men quit, finding the location too remote and the work boring. But two things about the memo stand out to Hollis. The first is that three men quit on the same day. The second is the date the men quit: March 12. The day the Van der Lip fell to pieces.

Hollis grabs a pen and writes down the men's names on a sheet of Department of Water stationery:

Helmer Berry
Frank Starbard
Chester Grunsky

The names don't mean anything to him, but that doesn't mean he didn't meet one or all of them at some point in time.

After a short knock his secretary enters with a sandwich and a cup of coffee on a tray. She sets the tray down on the edge of his desk.

Hollis ignores the food, digging back into the documents. It takes him half an hour to find addresses for all three men. One is in Hollywood, one's in Los Feliz, and the third's located at the northeast edge of the valley.

Satisfied, Hollis finally notices his lunch. Grabbing for the coffee, he discovers it's cold. He reaches for the sandwich instead and takes a bite. Chewing, he figures he can stop by two of the addresses after lunch. The one in the valley will have to wait until tomorrow.

Hollis drives up Vermont, heading to the address in Los Feliz for Helmer Berry. Hollis again tries to place the name, recall some sort of memory—a face, hair color, anything—but yet again he comes up blank.

Stopped behind a light at Sunset Boulevard, he sees the corner of Barnsdall Park on the northwest side of the street. Groups of men sit among the olive trees, huddling around small bonfires. Some play cards or throw dice. Others sleep, covered in newspapers. Hollis remembers when the park held billboards for Upton Sinclair in the 1934 governor's race. The cornerstone of Sinclair's platform was ending poverty in California. He didn't win.

Hollis passes the park and makes a right onto Franklin. Half a mile later, he turns left onto North Hoover. The building is on the corner, a white Spanish-style structure spanning three lots. The words EL MACANDO APARTMENTS are written in elegant script above an arched entrance. Roses and vines grow along the side of the building, partially obscuring the iron bars bolted to every window. A red FOR RENT sign is on the green lawn. Hollis parks around the corner.

Just inside the entrance, he spots a row of brass mailboxes. Hollis gets out the list of addresses he put together from the payroll files. *Helmer Berry, 1414 N. Hoover Apt. #8.* Squinting at the rows and rows of numbers in the dim light, he finds number eight. It says, in pencil, MONTANEZ. Hollis decides to check it out anyway.

The vestibule opens onto a courtyard, cool from the shade of the tall buildings on either side. Looking up, he sees black painted shutters, red terra-cotta tiles, and more vines clinging to the beige plaster. As he walks, he hears noises from inside the units. Babies crying, a couple fighting, a radio playing big band music. He finds number eight and knocks on the door.

Even though he can clearly hear sounds coming from inside the apartment, no one answers. Hollis knocks again, this time harder.

A minute later, the door opens a crack. A man's face, brown and sweaty.

"Oh, hello there, I'm looking for someone who used to live here. Do you think you can help me?"

The man just stares. Hollis continues.

"His name is Helmer Berry. Did you know him?"

"¿Quién eres tu? ¿Qué quieres?"

"Oh, Spanish." Hollis nervously adjusts his glasses. "Sir, do you by any chance speak English?"

"No hablo inglés. Dime qué quieres."

"Berry," Hollis repeats, enunciating each syllable, "Hel-mer... Berr-ree."

"Lo siento, señor, pero no sé nada."

The door slams closed.

Hollis lingers for a second, trying to remember the few Spanish phrases he had learned in the wake of Van der Lip. A large number of casualties came from Mexican families living near the Santa Clara River, and he'd tried to get information from the few survivors in the days after the disaster. But the only thing he can recall is how to ask, *How many people from your family are missing?*

Hollis turns and walks back through the courtyard. Passing by the mailboxes, he spots—at the very end and set apart from the others—the word MANAGER. He walks to the opposite side of the property, to where the manager's apartment is located near a covered garage. Hollis knocks.

The manager is short and tanned, his brown hair uncombed. He's wearing stained trousers and an undershirt that used to be white, but which is now yellow. Behind him, Hollis can see a row of keys hanging on nails.

"You come about the apartment?"

"Excuse me?"

The manager reaches for a set of keys.

"It's a lovely unit, has its own patio and everything. Let me show you."

"Sorry, no. I came for some information about a former tenant."

The manager shrugs and returns the keys.

"That's a shame. I'd love to get a few more people in here who speak English. These goddamn wetbacks, half the time I don't even know how many are in there."

"Helmer Berry," Hollis finally says. "Lived here about ten years ago. Unit number eight. Do you remember him?"

"Berry? Number eight?" He shakes his head and runs cigarette-stained fingers against his blond whiskers. "That's before my time, buddy. Two tenants ago it was a broad, and before that it was a colored fella. I wasn't too happy about that, either."

Hollis nods with his chin toward the manager's apartment.

"Would you have a forwarding address? In your records, maybe?"

The man laughs.

"I don't keep records like that. As long as people pay their rent, I don't ask too many questions."

"Well then, I thank you for your time."

"No problem. And you keep that apartment in mind, okay? We'd love to get a classy guy like yourself living here."

Hollis turns and leaves without saying goodbye.

Before getting into the Buick, he pulls out the list of

three addresses from his suit jacket. With his other hand he fishes for a pencil in his hip pocket. He crosses Helmer Berry off his list and slips the paper back into his pocket.

Hollis gets into the car, starts the engine, and drives toward Hollywood.

He pulls up to the address, a dark-brown bungalow located between Windsor and Plymouth. It's one of a dozen small houses on the short and quiet street. Just a few blocks away is the Wilshire Country Club and the mansions of Hancock Park, but here the homes are mainly one-story and modest. Hollis gets out of the Buick, double-checking the name on his list and the number on the curb. *Frank Starbard. 4750 West Fourth.* Approaching the house, he spots a blue Ford coupe in the driveway.

After Hollis rings the doorbell, he hears chimes echo throughout the house. He's about to ring again when the door is opened slowly by a woman. She's blonde and wears a red silk robe. She's young, barely thirty, and reminds him of Carole Lombard. He likes Carole Lombard.

"Can I help you?"

Her light-blue eyes are only half-open, like the door.

"Yes, I was—I'm looking for someone."

"I'd say you found someone."

Her voice is deep and smoky.

"No." Hollis blushes. "I mean a man. Frank Starbard. Do you know him?"

"I should hope so—he's my husband." She opens the door. "Would you like to come in?"

He hesitates for a moment before stepping inside.

She closes the door and leads Hollis to a living room with a beamed ceiling, leather couch, two velvet ottomans, and large windows covered by heavy green drapes. The warm air holds the stale smell of cigarettes.

"Care for a highball?"

"No, thank you." He looks at his watch. "It's a little early."

She smiles. "Then how about some iced tea?"

"That'll be fine."

She retreats to a kitchen Hollis can see through a doorway. Pale-yellow canisters, a shiny silver toaster, a can of Huggins-Young Coffee. As she opens cabinets and drawers, he also hears music coming from somewhere in the house.

"Sorry I'm not dressed," she calls out from the kitchen, "but I only just woke up. I work nights."

She reenters the room carrying the drinks in tall glasses with printed flowers.

"That must be hard," he says, "working nights, I mean."

She shrugs and hands one of the glasses to Hollis.

"With everything that's going on, I'm glad to have any old job."

She sits down. When she does, her robe falls open. She leaves it like that.

"Cheers."

He raises his glass and takes a sip. It's nothing but sugar.

"I'm sorry, Mister . . ." She trails off but then laughs. "I don't believe you've told me your name."

"Forgive me, Mrs. Starbard. My name is Mulwray. Hollis Mulwray."

"Pleased to meet you, Mr. Mulwray. My name is Sadie Royce."

"But you said Frank Starbard was . . ."

When he doesn't complete the thought, she does it for him.

"My husband? He is, but I kept my own name. Professional reasons." She opens a box on a coffee table and pulls out a long cigarette. She lights it. "You said you wanted to speak to Frank?"

"Yes, is he home?"

"I'm afraid I haven't seen Frank in seven months."

"I'm sorry to hear that."

She takes a deep drag on the cigarette and replies, "I'm not."

Hollis notices a picture frame on the mantel. She's

standing with a tall, dark-haired man. She's wearing a long, elegant dress, and he has on a pin-striped suit. The picture looks to have been taken in a nightclub. Behind them is a jazz band. Hollis points with the hand that's holding the drink.

"Is that him?"

"Yes, up in San Francisco. That's where I'm from."

Hollis approaches the photo to examine it more closely. He scans the man's face, trying to place it on someone he might have come across all those years ago at the dam. The man's wearing a funny grin, and his eyes seem hard and cruel. Hollis turns back to Sadie.

"Has he left town?"

She takes a sip of the iced tea before answering.

"I'm afraid you might need to tell me what this is all about, Mr. Mulwray, before I divulge any more private details."

"Yes, of course, Mrs. Royce," Hollis says. "You see, I'm with the water department."

She tilts her head and examines him.

"You look too dry to be in water." She takes another drag on her cigarette. "I think it's the bow tie."

"Your husband"—Hollis blushes again—"used to work for the water department. At a dam, north of the city. Back in the '20s."

"Frank performed *honest* work? I had no idea."

"He never spoke of it?"

"When I met him, he was in a different line altogether."

"And what was that, if you don't mind my asking?"

"Show business. He saw me singing in a joint and offered to be my manager. That's why I moved down here."

He takes a small sip and asks, "To be with him?"

She smiles and replies, "To be in pictures."

"And how does that—did that work out?"

"Not so good. Not *yet*, anyway." She takes a final drag of the cigarette and stubs it out. "Frank got me a few bit parts here and there, but nothing to write home about. Now that he's skipped town, I'm back to doing what I did before I met him."

"And what's that?"

"Singing. I'm the warm-up act at the Cocoanut Grove."

"The Ambassador Hotel, right?"

She nods.

"I'm the entertainment when people are eating. It gets livelier later on, but at seven you're just crooning to a whole lot of men and their meals. Sometimes I think they like the lobster casserole more than they like me."

When she crosses her legs, the robe falls open even more.

"You say your husband's no longer in Los Angeles, Mrs. Royce?"

"Call me Sadie. And that's right, Mr. Mulwray."

"Do you happen to know where he went?"

"To get a pack of cigarettes." She laughs. "I guess he got lost."

Hollis takes another sip of the tea and then sets the glass down on the coffee table.

"Are there any friends or acquaintances I might be able to follow up with?"

She shakes her head. When she does, a tuft of blonde hair falls from behind an ear and covers half her face.

"Frank was a loner. Never had many friends, as far as I could tell." She nods toward the back of the house. "I put a few of his things in a closet if you'd like to take a look. There might be an address book or some papers that could help."

Hollis begins to feel himself sweat.

"Don't worry, Mr. Mulwray." She smiles. "It's not in the bedroom."

Sadie gets up and walks toward the back of the house. Hollis reluctantly follows.

Along a hallway with three doors, she points to the one in the middle.

"I'll leave you to it. When you're done, come find me."

Hollis nods and she retreats back to the living room. As she walks, the hem of the red robe wafts back and forth like a swing. Hollis opens the door.

It's a nondescript guest room. Twin bed, end table,

lamp, alarm clock. The walls are bare. Hollis opens the closet. There are half a dozen suits, four white shirts, and a few pairs of worn leather shoes. One of the suits is the pin-striped one from the photo on the mantel. On the floor, next to a homemade shoeshine kit, is an orange crate filled with papers. Hollis picks up the wooden box and puts it on the bed. When he sits down to examine the papers, the bed's rusted springs creak.

Most of the papers are bills, all of them past due. Flipping past these, he comes across a copy of *Racing Form* from last year, the banner headline declaring "Seabiscuit Takes Bay Meadows by Five Lengths." Underneath this, Hollis finds a series of pamphlets. *Socialism: True and False. Wrongs That Require Remedies. Chants for Socialists.* At the very bottom of the crate are two tin buttons. One features a black-and-white photo of a man in profile, the words JACOB HOKE SOCIALIST CANDIDATE FOR MAYOR wrapped around the edge. The other says LOS ANGELES 1929 FOR THE WORKERS. Hollis thinks back to the Van der Lip. There had been talk at the time that anarchists or communists might have been the ones to dynamite the dam.

Hollis takes the two buttons, returns the rest of the papers, and puts the orange crate back into the closet.

Exiting the room, he looks down the hallway. The door to the master bedroom is open. He sees a large unmade bed with blue satin sheets. Hollis turns and walks back toward the living room. Sadie's sitting in the same chair, smoking another cigarette. Along with the smoke, there's a new scent in the air. Perfume. Lilacs.

"Find anything?"

He holds up the buttons.

"Just these."

"Oh, *him*." She points with the cigarette. "Frank worked for Hoke. On the election."

"As what, a campaign volunteer?"

"Something like that." She takes a drag on the cigarette and exhales. Now there's less perfume in the room. "They were close for a time, but something happened. I don't know what."

"Do you mind if I keep them?"

She shrugs.

Putting the buttons in his pocket, he asks, "Do you think Frank will ever come back?"

"He'll be back. The bigger question is whether or not I'll be here when that happens."

"Where would you go?"

"Maybe back to San Francisco. Or out to New York. I've never been, have you?"

"New York? Yes, many times."

"Is it glamorous? I'd love to go to all of the shows and the fancy restaurants. Los Angeles is nice and all, but it's no Manhattan."

Hollis glances at his watch. It's nearly two.

"I should be going, Mrs. Royce. I've taken up too much of your time."

She gets up and approaches him. He wants to step back but doesn't.

"I told you, call me Sadie."

"Yes," he says, blushing for the third time.

"Mr. Mulwray, may I ask you something?"

"Yes, of course."

"Would you come and see me sing sometime?"

"I just—I don't know if I should."

She places both her hands on his hands. Hers are smooth and soft. His begin to tremble.

"I'm still new to LA, and I don't know many people. I'd like to have a friend in the audience."

He looks into her eyes. They're the color of the morning sky. There's a flaw in one of Evelyn's eyes, but Sadie doesn't have a single flaw that Hollis can see.

"Cocoanut Grove. Every night at seven, except on Monday."

"Every night at seven," he repeats.

"Except on Monday," she adds, grinning.

He takes his hands back.

"I'll try, Mrs. Royce." He walks to the front door. "Thank you again for your time."

She calls after him, "You're quite welcome, Mr. Mulwray."

When he gets back to the Buick, he sits for a moment.

Traffic passes by in both directions, but Hollis doesn't move. He just stays there, raises his hands, and smells her perfume on his skin. Lilacs.

Back at the office, it takes him three tries to wash the smell of Sadie off his hands. He wanted to stop after two tries, to leave at least a hint of the scent, but his secretary shot him such a look when he first returned, Hollis thought it better to remove all trace.

Now, as he's seated behind his desk, he takes out the piece of paper with the names and addresses. Last on the list is Chester Grunsky. The address is in San Fernando. There's not much out there but orchards and a few farms. It's almost as desolate as what he saw yesterday in Chatsworth.

Hollis is about to put the list back into his pocket when he grabs a pen and writes, next to Frank Starbard's name, *Cocoanut Grove, except on Mondays*. When he puts the pen back in its holder, he sees a picture of Evelyn that sits on the corner of the desk. It's a hand-tinted photo of his wife in her riding clothes. Brown breeches, hunter-green coat, black helmet. Smile. Hollis sniffs and can still smell the faintest trace of lilac. As he reaches for the silver frame, giving it a half-turn so that the photo is facing the other way, there's a knock on the hallway door.

"Come in."

The door opens. Elwin Ransome stands with a handful of papers. Just like yesterday, he's wearing a collared shirt with rolled-up sleeves.

"Good afternoon, Elwin. How can I help you?"

"Mr. Mulwray, do you have a few minutes?"

"Of course." As he waves Elwin toward the chair in front of his desk, Hollis hides the list of addresses underneath a pile of documents that require his signature. "What is it?"

"Well, sir, after the discussion with you and Mr. Yelburton, about the threats to the reservoirs, I thought I'd pull the logs for the past couple of weeks and take a look at the levels."

"And what did you find?"

Elwin hands Hollis the papers.

"They're low, almost all of them. Much lower than they should be."

Hollis's eyes begin to scan across the rows of numbers.

"Well, Elwin, there's a drought. Of course they're—"

"I realize that, Mr. Mulwray. But *those* numbers"—he points to the papers—"aren't consistent with water loss due to increased usage, heat, or the lack of annual rainfall. We have models for all of that, and the current capacity—

across the city—doesn't come close. Here, I computed it myself."

He pulls out of his pocket a piece of graph paper folded into fourths. The sheet is covered with data.

"This is where the reservoirs *should* be. The figures in the reports are way off."

Hollis compares the two, looking back and forth like he's watching a tennis match.

"Someone's dumping water," Ransome finally says.

"Wait a minute, Elwin. Let's not jump to conclusions. Russ mentioned water was indeed being diverted. To farmers in the valley, he said. If that's the case, there'd be a bit of runoff."

"I realize that, Mr. Mulwray. But we'd be having to irrigate half the state to deplete the reservoirs *that* much."

As Hollis continues to scrutinize the figures, the engineer says, more to himself than to Hollis, "Why, if the papers got hold of this."

"I know, Elwin," Hollis says slowly. "The bond issue would be assured and I'd have no choice but to build the Vallejo dam."

Hollis gets up and walks to a bookshelf stuffed with thick volumes. *The Design and Construction of Dams. Masonry Dam Design.* He pulls down a huge collection of maps and blueprints for all the aqueducts, dams, and reservoirs in the area. Dropping it to the conference room table, it lands with a thump. WATERSHED AND

DRAINAGE SYSTEM FOR THE LOS ANGELES BASIN is stamped in gold on the black leather cover. Hollis opens to the pages for the Oak Pass Reservoir.

"What are you going to do, Mr. Mulwray?"

"I'm going to do a little digging." He looks up from the book and calls over his shoulder, "Thank you for bringing this to my attention."

Elwin nods and leaves the office. Hollis retrieves from his desk the reports and Elwin's numbers. He's comparing the figures to the plans in the book when he hears footsteps and voices in the vestibule between his office and Yelburton's.

"Hollis, do you have a minute?"

He looks up to see Russ standing in the doorway next to a stocky man in a rumpled suit, short tie, and a stained shirt. An unlit cigarette dangles from his lips. Yelburton is, as usual, dressed impeccably in a light-gray suit and purple tie. Not a hair out of place.

"Sure, Russ, what is it?"

"I'd like to introduce you to Claude Mulvihill. I've just hired him to be in charge of security for the reservoirs."

Hollis walks across the office to shake hands. Mulvihill's hand is flabby, his grip almost nonexistent.

"Hollis Mulwray, pleased to meet you."

Claude just grunts. Hollis sniffs and can smell gin.

"Claude and his men should be in place in just a few days. Isn't that right, Claude?"

He grunts again.

"Well, let me just say thank you for your efforts," Hollis says, "and if there's anything you or your men need, just let us know."

Mulvihill nods but doesn't say anything. Russ leads him back to the vestibule and closes the door. They hear him grunt goodbye to the secretary.

Once Hollis is sure Mulvihill is gone, he speaks.

"Russ, are you sure about this?"

"He comes highly recommended, I assure you."

"Yes, but—"

"We need boots on the ground, Hollis. That's all it is. If they see something, they'll phone it in. We'll take it from there."

"Fine, but let's keep them on a short leash."

"Of course."

After Russ returns to his office, Hollis retrieves the big book from his conference table and brings it to his desk. As he's pushing aside a pile of files to make space, he sees a square of paper. It says MAYOR with a phone number underneath. He picks up the phone to speak to his secretary.

"Yes, Mr. Mulwray?"

"I see that the mayor called. Did McCauley say what he wanted?"

"No, he didn't, sir. And it was the *ex*-mayor who phoned, not McCauley."

"Sam Bagby?"
"Yes, sir."
"Thank you, Oramae."

He hangs up the phone and looks at the number. MU 2779. Hollis crumples the paper and tosses it in a wastebasket that sits beside the tall desk.

3

THE NEXT MORNING, after another night filled with dark visions of water and death, Hollis wakes earlier than usual. Turning, he sees Evelyn. Her caramel-colored hair is splayed across the white pillow. She's still asleep. Hollis slips out of bed, showers, shaves.

Entering the kitchen from the back stairs, he surprises two female servants preparing breakfast. One of them has been with the house since they bought it. The other is young and seems unsure of herself. She moves with quick, nervous movements, looking to the other for approval.

They both have the same deep-set features and skin the shade of weak tea. Hollis suspects she's the daughter.

"*¿Café?*"

"Yes, please, just coffee. I'll take it outside."

Hollis walks through the kitchen to the dining room, heading for the iron table and chairs on the veranda.

The morning is cool, the sky slightly overcast. The sun is hidden behind clouds. Maybe it won't be so hot today, the heat finally breaking. It's quiet and all Hollis can hear are birds. Closing his eyes, he smells lilacs. His mind wanders. Sadie. Cocoanut Grove. Every night except Monday. He tries to remember what today is. It's Thursday.

The younger woman delivers the coffee on a silver platter along with three newspapers. He smiles at her as she places everything on the table, but she keeps her head down, focused on the task.

Hollis sips his coffee and flips through the papers. The local headlines are the usual. Drought, unemployment, heat. Nationally, things aren't much better. "Residents of Midwest Choke in Big Dust Storm." "More Banks Close in New York City." It's bad all over.

Flipping through the *Examiner*, he comes across another editorial about the dam. "We Need Water Now." He doesn't recognize the writer's name, Alistair Dill. A drawing of sand pouring out of a faucet labeled LOS ANGELES accompanies the article. Hollis is running out of time, and he knows it.

He finishes his coffee and heads back inside the house. It's quiet. Evelyn must still be asleep. Hollis decides to let her rest. He grabs his hat and heads for the Buick.

On the way downtown, at the corner of Temple and Grand, he passes an abandoned construction site. Hollis has been driving this way for years and has never seen a man anywhere near the large lot. It was going to be apartments, before the money ran out. Now it's just the ghost of a structure that will never be built.

In the 1920s, it was the opposite. Construction was everywhere. You couldn't drive down the street without seeing huge cranes and dozens of men in hard hats, sweating from their efforts. Cement mixers and trucks filled with lumber mixed with evening rush-hour traffic. Jackhammers were a constant noise in the background.

Back then, lured by the promise of paradise and opportunity, people moved to the city in droves. This meant new homes, schools, office buildings, warehouses, stores. Once the stock market crashed, all of that stopped. City blocks became like photographs, never changing, held in time. Nobody built anything new, and what already existed began to fade and crumble.

People still move to California—almost a thousand arrive every day—only now they're spurred on by death and desperation. They come from dust bowl states in jalopies with mattresses and chairs strapped to battered fenders and steaming hoods. By the time they discover

Los Angeles isn't the paradise they expected, they don't have the means to leave.

At the office, his secretary gives him a funny look when he arrives.

"You're in awfully early, Mr. Mulwray."

"Thought I'd get an early start since I'll be out most of the day."

She follows him into his office, carrying a stack of messages and letters.

"Sam Bagby called again."

Hollis ignores this. He takes the papers and sits down at his desk.

"Anything from Ransome?"

"Elwin? No," she answers, "should there be?"

Hollis shakes his head.

She returns to her desk as he digs into the papers. For a few hours he answers letters, signs documents, and returns phone calls. He'd hoped to be in the valley by noon but, at this rate, he won't make it until after one. His secretary orders him lunch again. He eats while he works, trying to save time.

He's just finishing a club sandwich when he comes across the letter. Before he even unfolds it, he knows what it is. The heavy white paper folded into thirds.

IF YOU BUILD THE DAM YOU DIE, MULWRAY

He picks up the phone.

"Oramae, could you come in here?"

When she arrives, he hands her the note. Her already-pale face becomes somehow even more white.

"It was in with my regular mail, and yet it doesn't have a postmark. Did you see who delivered it?"

She looks from the letter to him.

"Delivered? Why, sir, I believe it came with the regular mail."

While he's considering this, she continues.

"Do you want me to call the detective?"

Hollis takes back the note.

"We don't have anything more to go on than we did the other day. We'd just be wasting his time."

"But"—she points to the letter—"they're naming you, Mr. Mulwray. It's a direct threat."

"I'm the chief engineer, Oramae. Who else are they going to threaten?"

She's about to speak again when he cuts her off. "You may return to your desk."

"Please, Mr. Mulwray, I'm *begging* you."

"That's quite enough, Oramae."

Grumbling, she exits the office and slams the door.

Even though he'd acted nonchalant with his secretary, the letter indeed makes him uneasy. First the nightmares, and now this. Hollis feels like something bad is getting closer. He quickly opens a drawer and adds the note to the others.

By the time he finishes the paperwork, it's half past one. Reaching into his pocket, he retrieves the piece of paper from yesterday with the three names and addresses. Chester Grunsky is last on the list. San Fernando.

In the vestibule, his secretary picks at a tuna salad sandwich.

"Goodbye, Oramae. I'll be out in the field for the remainder of the day."

"Did you at least return Sam Bagby's call, Mr. Mulwray?"

Hollis grins as he leaves.

The valley is even hotter today than it was earlier in the week. It must be a hundred degrees. Hollis has to constantly wipe the sweat from his forehead as he drives. At one point, he pulls over to take off his suit jacket.

The address leads him to a small farm in the foothills of mountains covered in dry brush. The crops surrounding the property look just as dry. Hollis parks the Buick next to a dented mailbox attached to a leaning wooden post. Getting out of the car, he rolls up his shirtsleeves.

A long dirt driveway leads to a barn that used to be red but is now more of a faded orange. Farming equipment—tractor, plough, a machine with gears and a chute Hollis doesn't recognize—stands rusted along the path. A white clapboard house leans opposite the barn. In between the house and the barn, half a dozen men in overalls are gathered around a green pickup truck that's seen better days. The faces look as dirty and beat-up as the truck. Hollis approaches.

"Chester Grunsky?"

The small crowd slowly turns, and one of the men steps forward. He's wearing soiled work clothes, worn boots, and a sweat-stained cowboy hat.

"Can I talk to you? My name is—"

"I know who ya are."

The men standing around the truck go back to what they were doing as Chester walks toward the rusted tractor. Hollis follows.

"Mulwray, right?" he says, leaning against a huge rubber tire caked in dirt. "You're from the water department."

Hollis is somewhat taken aback.

"Have we met?"

"No, but I worked out at the Van der Lip." Grunsky smiles wide. "You don't remember me?"

"Should I?"

The man spits tobacco into the dirt.

"No, I guess not. I was just another pitman."

"How long did you work at the dam?"

"Years. Was there when it was built, stayed for a job after."

"What had you done before that?"

"Apricot ranch up north. Got paid twenty cents an hour for ten-hour days." He laughs darkly. "For some reason, I thought working for the water department would be easier. It wasn't."

The aqueduct, reservoirs, and dams were purposefully built away from towns and cities. This meant the men who built them had to live in tents, out in the middle of nowhere. The food was bad. It was too hot during the day and too cold at night. For months, the only thing to do after hours was gamble or drink.

"You quit the day the dam failed. Why?"

Hollis watches the man's face closely.

"I'd been meaning to quit for weeks, but the paycheck always seemed to make me stay."

"So then why did you finally quit? And why on that particular day?"

Chester shrugs.

"Heard a couple of fellas talk about leaving. One of them had a car. I asked if they'd give me a ride and they said yes."

"You didn't know them before that?"

"Seen one of 'em around. Had never talked to him, but his face was familiar."

"Which was that?" Hollis retrieves the list from his pants pocket. "Frank Starbard or Helmer Berry?"

Chester looks up at the sun and squints.

"Can't remember. Like I said, I didn't know his name."

Hollis puts the list back into his pocket.

"Where did you all go once you left the dam?"

"Thought they were just headed into Newhall, but they drove all the way down to Los Angeles. When they stopped at some place downtown to get a bite to eat, I left."

"Did they say anything on the drive? Talk about the dam, or their plans?"

Chester thinks back.

"Not that I can recall. Anyway, I was in the back seat and may not have heard. It was a hot day, the windows were down."

"Did they have any bags with them? Luggage?"

Hollis is trying to figure out whether the men left on the spur of the moment and, if not, whether their departure—and thus the attack on the dam—had been pre-planned.

Again, Chester just shakes his head.

"Not that I could see, but they maybe had some bags in the trunk."

"How about you?"

"No, sir. All I had was the shirt on my back and a satchel stuffed with rags."

Behind them the truck, now laden with men, starts up. The engine groans and backfires as it lurches along the dirt path to the road. Chester gives the driver a weary half wave as it passes.

"What did you think the next day?" Hollis says.

"About what?"

"When you'd heard the dam had failed."

"Thought I'd gotten lucky." He spits at the ground again. "And that all those poor bastards back in the canyon weren't."

As Hollis considers all of this, Chester speaks.

"Now can I ask *you* a question, Mr. Mulwray?"

"Of course."

"How do you do it? Taking something that don't belong to you and making decisions about who gets to make a living and who don't."

"My job, Mr. Grunksy, is to move water from where it is to where it isn't."

Chester looks around at his arid crops.

"Well, it sure ain't here, Mr. Mulwray."

Hollis pushes up his glasses from where they'd slipped down his nose.

"I'm sorry, Mr. Grunsky, but the city needs drinking water. That means cutbacks. Rationing is the only way."

"What's the point of having water to drink, if people like me don't have food to eat?"

"I'm sorry you see it that way. The goal of the water

department is to do the greatest good for the greatest number of people. Why, large-scale waterworks have been crucial to man's survival for six thousand years."

Chester smiles again.

"Well, I don't know about six thousand years, but I've been doing my best out here for a decade to grow lima beans, walnuts, and lemons, and I don't got a pot to piss in."

"Times are hard for everyone."

Chester looks Hollis up and down.

"Don't look like they're hard for you."

Hollis takes a paisley handkerchief out of his pocket and wipes down his forehead. He instantly regrets this. The handkerchief is made of silk.

"I believe I've taken up enough of your time. Thank you for answering my questions, Mr. Grunsky."

Hollis begins to walk back to the Buick, but Chester grabs his arm to stop him.

"Wait a minute, Mr. Mulwray. You came all the way out here to ask me about the dam. You think I had something to do with it?"

"You quit the day it came down. You and those two other men. You don't think that looks suspicious?"

"I guess that could look like a lot of things." Chester spits again. "But that don't make any of them true."

Hollis holds the man's gaze for a moment before turning and heading back to the Buick.

After getting into the car, Hollis slams the steering wheel. Another dead end.

Instead of going back to the office, he decides to traverse the length of the valley and head out to the coast. His plan is to visit his mom in Santa Monica and then have an early dinner at the Cocoanut Grove.

As he drives, Hollis passes empty lot after empty lot littered with SOLD signs. In a huge field, a man stands in front of a billboard that says $25 AN ACRE. The man is hanging a bright-red SALE PENDING sign from the billboard.

This makes no sense; land around here is worthless. Chester Grunsky's small stake, even with the structures and failing crops, would barely be worth twenty dollars an acre. So why is someone paying more than that for just dirt?

Hollis shakes his head and keeps on driving.

The visitor parking lot at the rest home is never crowded. Holidays might see it half-full, and on Christmas there's often just two or three free spaces, but on most days there's not more than one car. Today it's empty until Hollis shows up.

As he parks, he feels the usual guilt begin to set in.

They have more than enough room at the house, and there are servants to wait on his mother hand and foot. Evelyn even grudgingly agreed to her living there years ago. But his mother has constantly refused, offering various excuses. Hollis knows the real reason. She doesn't approve of Evelyn. Even more, she doesn't approve of Katherine.

Hollis gets out of the Buick. Walking to the front entrance, he looks down and can see the Pacific Coast Highway. The rest home is high on a hill, overlooking the ocean. It's a clear afternoon, and Hollis can see all the way to Catalina. This makes him think of Noah Cross, so he looks away.

Signing in at the front desk, he tries to think back. When was the last time he was here? His mother's birthday is in May, but he hopes it wasn't that long ago. He grins, figuring she'll remind him.

Beyond the entrance there's a large room where residents gather to play bingo and make quilts. On Saturday nights they have dancing, and out back there's a shuffleboard court. There are all kinds of activities, but whenever he asks his mom about them, she claims to never take part. "I keep to myself," she tells him.

Her room is located around the back. Unlike most units, which look onto an inner courtyard, he pays extra so his mother can have an ocean view. He knocks twice lightly and enters.

She's in a wheelchair, a blanket across her lap. She has trouble walking so, when she's not in bed, she rests in the chair. Someone comes for her three times a day to bring her to the main hall for meals. She smiles brightly when she registers who it is.

"Hollis! It's so good to see you."

He leans in to kiss her on the cheek.

"Good to see you too, Mama."

He takes off his hat and sits down on a wooden chair opposite the bed.

"How are you, Mama? Are you feeling better?"

"Oh, yes. The cough I had is almost completely gone. And the doctor said it wasn't pneumonia after all, just a bad cold."

"I'm glad to hear that."

"And how about you, Son? Is everything okay?"

"Yes, Mama, I'm fine."

"And your wife, how is she?"

"Keeping busy, as usual. Lunches with friends. Dinner parties. You know Evelyn."

She replies, her voice dark, "Yes, I know Evelyn."

He changes the subject.

"Did you get the book I sent?"

She points to the Agatha Christie novel on her nightstand. *Dumb Witness*.

"Yes, thank you, Son. You know how much I love a good mystery."

"I do, Mama."

As she readjusts the blanket on her lap, he looks around the room. It's clean, but bare. The rooms are all furnished, but residents are allowed and even encouraged to bring in their own items in order to make themselves feel more at home.

When he moved her down here four years ago, all she brought were two suitcases. Hollis managed to keep a few pieces of furniture from the house in Monterey, along with a handful of mementos, but the rest of it—the house and everything in it—was sold.

The only personal item in the room is a photo, a faded shot of his father as a young man. Hollis looks a lot like him. They have the same pointed nose and bowed shoulders.

His father died young at the age of fifty-three. There had been few warning signs. Hollis wouldn't have taken the job in Los Angeles, let alone have been in a remote part of the state working on the aqueduct, if he knew his father was seriously ill. As soon as word got to him, Hollis rushed back to Monterey. His father's finances were a mess, with debts owed. It took Hollis months to sort everything out, and years to pay it all off.

"Are you happy here, Mama? I've told you before, you're welcome to live with us."

"No, Hollis"—she waves him off—"I don't want to be a burden. Besides, I like it here. The smell of the ocean reminds me of Monterey. Remember when you were a boy, the tide pools?"

He nods his head slowly.

"I remember, Mama."

She closes her eyes and leans back.

"You and your father would be out there for hours. If it wasn't for the tide coming in, you'd have been out there all night."

"Papa loved staring at the sea life."

She opens her eyes.

"*You* loved staring at the sea life, Hollis. Your father just liked being with you." She smiles and touches his hand. "He would have been proud to see what you've become."

His father had been a dreamer, never very successful in business. As a boy he'd heard the rags-to-riches stories of California. How penniless prospectors made millions, first in gold in 1849 and then, just a decade later, in silver. After the transcontinental railroad was completed in 1869, land became the next precious commodity. Hollis's father, as a young man, tried to take part. He borrowed money and bought plots in new towns like Gladysta, Irvington, Drew. His plan was to buy as much as he could, hold on to the land until it increased in value, and then double if not triple his money. In 1886 he met Hollis's mother. She was from a respectable family, the daughter of a banker. This assured access to more money. It ended in catastrophe. By 1888 the land boom collapsed, and Hollis's father lost everything. Humiliated, they moved to Monterey and he found a job at a dry goods store. He went from land speculation to stocking shelves. By the time Hollis was born in 1892, he had risen to manager. At one point there was an opportunity to buy out the owner, but Hollis's father had no credit and had run out of influence with his wife's family. He remained someone else's employee until the day he died.

"I'm glad to hear that, Mama. I think of Papa often."

She turns and looks at the photo.

"I do, too, Hollis."

"Do you need anything? Something for your room maybe?"

"No," she says slowly, her eyes again closing. "They take good care of me here."

He doesn't say anything. After a few seconds, she nods off. Hollis lets her sleep. Above her faint snore, he hears the ocean, waves breaking on the shoreline. He looks at his watch. The Cocoanut Grove will be open soon.

Ten minutes later, she pops awake and asks, "How long was I out for?"

"Not long, Mama, but I should go."

"Hollis, you just got here."

"I know, Mama, but I'm busy. I'll stop by again soon. Next week, I promise."

He grabs his hat.

"You be safe, Hollis. I worry about you."

"Why would you worry about me?"

"Newspapers get left in the main room. I see your name from time to time. I don't like the things they say about you."

"Don't mind the newspapers, I can handle it. They're just trying to put pressure on me to build the new dam."

She reaches out for his hands. Hers feel like brittle paper.

"I don't want you to die young, like your father."

"I'm not going to die, Mama." He takes back his hands and brushes a strand of gray hair out of her face. "I'm going to grow nice and old, just like you."

"Promise me you'll be safe, Hollis. Promise me you won't take any foolish risks."

He looks her in the eye. Her brown eyes are dulled and rheumy. He wonders how much time she has left.

"I promise, Mama."

He gives her another kiss on the cheek and walks back to the entrance. There's a young brunette behind the front desk he's never seen before.

"May I use your telephone?"

"Of course."

He picks up the receiver and dials his home. The butler answers.

"Good evening, Khan, this is Mr. Mulwray."

"You want to talk to Mrs. Mulwray?"

"No, thank you. Just tell her I won't be home for dinner. I have a business engagement."

"Yes, sir. Is that all?"

"That is all, thank you, Khan."

He hangs up the phone and heads out to the parking lot. His car is still the only car there.

The Ambassador Hotel sits on a huge plot of land, taking up two city blocks south of Wilshire. The expansive grounds contain a four-hundred-room hotel, a nightclub, a restaurant, dozens of stand-alone bungalows, and a lawn larger than a football field. Hollis pulls into the driveway and stops under the white circular awning that extends over the entrance. He stops the car but leaves the engine running. A valet runs up, hands him a ticket, and drives off with the Buick as Hollis enters the building.

The lobby holds a gigantic Italian fireplace that is thankfully dormant since the night has not yet turned cool, the sun only recently setting. Ornate chandeliers hang from the ceiling and intricate draperies cover every wall. Down a long corridor Hollis sees the entrance to the Cocoanut Grove. Just beyond that, there's a single door marked ARTISTS' ENTRANCE. He opens one of the two glass doors covered in a green-and-brown painting of palm trees and descends down a staircase with shag carpet so thick he feels like he's walking on sand.

The huge space is made to look like a jungle. Large palm fronds are everywhere, along with papier-mâché coconuts and stuffed monkeys with yellow light-bulb eyes that blink in the half dark. On the ceiling is a mural of the night sky. A maître d' clutching a pile of menus meets Hollis at the bottom of the stairs.

"Good evening, sir. How many in your party?"

"Just one, please."

The room is not even a quarter full, so the maître d' gives him a table up front. The stage is just fifteen feet away. Hollis reads the band name on the dozen music stands lining the stage. BUNNY BERIGAN AND HIS ORCHESTRA.

"Hello, sir, welcome to the world-famous Cocoanut Grove. Can I get you started with a cocktail?"

Hollis looks up. The waitress, a brunette, is older—she's almost Hollis's age.

"Oh, well, I—what do you recommend?"

"Our prize-winning drinks are the Merry K Cocktail and the Cocoanut Grove Cooler."

When he doesn't respond, she continues.

"Or how about a martini, vodka daiquiri, or Manhattan?"

"The vodka," he says, absentmindedly.

She nods and walks to another table that has also just

been seated. Hollis hears her repeat the same welcome and drink suggestions.

After the waitress is gone, Hollis glances around. He's looking for Sadie, but also trying not to stand out. Evelyn has friends everywhere. All he sees are couples and groups of men—probably business dinners—seated throughout the room.

The waitress returns quickly with the cocktail. Hollis takes a sip and winces. He should have ordered an old-fashioned.

"And for dinner?"

He glances down at the menu and chooses the first thing he sees.

"Uh, the Chicken Cocoanut Grove, please."

"Excellent choice."

As she scribbles down his order on a notepad and moves to the next table, Hollis looks at his watch. The show should be starting soon.

"Why, Mr. Mulwray."

He turns to see Sadie standing by the side of the table. She's wearing a dark-red gown and a string of pearls. The top of her hair is combed flat, but the ends are curled. Her lips are painted the same deep red of her dress.

"Mrs. Royce, hello."

"I told you, Mr. Mulwray, call me Sadie." She motions to the table. "May I join you?"

"Of course. Would you like something to drink?"

"Well, the manager frowns on it."

"I'd hate to get you into trouble."

Sitting down, she says, "What *would* you like to get me into?"

Grinning, Hollis waves down the waitress.

"Hello, Sadie."

Sadie looks up and regards the waitress warily.

"Hello, Ida. Whiskey and soda, when you have a chance."

The waitress leaves.

"God," Sadie says under her breath, "I can't stand some of the older girls. They didn't make it back in the silent era, and now they're taking it out on all of us young gals."

The waitress returns with the drink and drops it off without a word. Hollis and Sadie sip their cocktails.

Not knowing what to say, Hollis points with his drink to the stage.

"That Bunny Berigan, is he good?"

She chuckles.

"Yeah, but he's a drunk. Doesn't even bother to show up for my show. Probably hasn't woken up yet from last night." She inches closer to him. "I'm glad you came."

He takes a sip of his drink to hide the fact that he's blushing.

"I just hope," she continues, "that this is a social visit."

"What do you mean?"

"Well, are you interested in me or in Frank?"

He doesn't know how to reply. Yes, he's still trying to get answers about the dam, but that's not why he's here.

He's about to answer when she takes his arm in order to look at his watch.

"Jesus, I'm late."

She downs the whiskey in one gulp and stands up.

"Stay and talk to me after?"

"Oh, I'm—I can't, not tonight."

She seems hurt.

"Maybe tomorrow?"

"Yes," he says, smiling and repeating, "maybe tomorrow."

She gives him a kiss on the cheek. When she does, he's enveloped by her perfume. Lilacs.

She winks and disappears around the side of the stage.

Hollis is still smiling when the waitress brings him his dinner.

"Chicken Cocoanut Grove. Enjoy."

He looks down to see a coconut sitting on a plate. The coconut is hollowed out and inside is some sort of chicken stew. When he leans down to smell the stew, he sees that the coconut is on a bed of white rice. The stew smells of curry and onions.

He's picking at his meal when men in tuxedoes begin to take their seats on the bandstand. The lights in the room dim and a voice announces, "Ladies and gentlemen, please welcome to the stage, the lovely Sadie Royce."

He pushes aside the plate and watches Sadie walk onto the stage to polite applause.

"Good evening, everyone. Here's a song I hope comes true soon. It's called 'September in the Rain.'"

There are scattered chuckles and more half-hearted clapping as the band members pick up their instruments and begin playing.

Sadie closes her eyes and sways to the music. When she sings, her voice is flat and breathy.

"To every word of love I heard you whisper, the raindrops seemed to play a sweet refrain."

It's not a great voice, but Hollis still can't take his eyes off her.

"Though spring is here, to me it's still September. That September in the rain."

No one in the room seems to be paying her much attention. People are talking and eating loudly. Hollis can hear laughter and discussions; Sadie's performance might as well be wallpaper. Hollis doesn't care. He tunes out all the distractions and focuses on her. The waitress returns and Hollis orders another daiquiri, just to be able to stay and watch Sadie sing.

After another couple of songs, he looks at his watch. He'd better be getting home. Evelyn will be wondering where he is.

Hollis stands up, pulls a twenty-dollar bill out of his wallet, lays it on the table. As he's leaving, he turns to get a last look. Sadie spots him and gives a wink as she introduces "I've Got You Under My Skin."

He smiles all the way home.

Entering the house, Hollis immediately senses that something is different. He spots two trunks and a set of matching luggage stacked in the foyer opposite the coat closet. The luggage—slate gray with shiny chrome clasps—looks vaguely familiar. Leaning down, he reads the monogram. KAM. A cold chill comes over him. Any warmth he'd brought from the Cocoanut Grove immediately disappears.

"Papa?"

He looks from the luggage to a young woman standing in the hallway. She's wearing a light-blue dress and black Mary Janes with a small heel, and her white-blonde hair is pulled back on both sides with bobby pins.

"Katherine."

As he takes off his hat and leans in to give her a kiss, Evelyn joins them.

"I picked her up at the train station an hour ago."

Hollis tries to hide both his shock and his displeasure.

"But, Evelyn . . . why didn't you tell me?"

She takes the girl's hand.

"We wanted it to be a surprise."

Evelyn turns and leads the way to the living room. She sits on the couch and retrieves a lit cigarette from an ashtray. A half-empty highball glass is next to a crystal bowl filled with matchsticks. Katherine is perched in a large wingback chair next to where a glass of milk rests on an end table.

Hollis joins his wife on the couch as the butler follows them into the room.

"A drink perhaps, Mr. Mulwray?"

"Yes, Khan, thank you. An old-fashioned."

After the butler leaves, Hollis says to Katherine, "How long will you be staying, sweetheart?"

"Gee, I don't know." She looks to Evelyn. "We didn't talk about that."

Evelyn takes a drag from her cigarette and blows smoke toward the ceiling.

"It was all a bit spur of the moment, darling, but we'll figure it out."

Katherine turns back to Hollis.

"Wait until you hear my Spanish, Papa. I've been working really hard. My teacher says I speak it better than the locals. And my writing's gotten better, too."

"That's wonderful, sweetheart. I'm so proud."

The butler returns with the drink, bending at the waist. He's leaving, the tray tucked under his arm, when Evelyn calls after him.

"Khan, would you please show Katherine to her room? I'd like for her to be in the guest room right across from us."

"Yes, ma'am." He turns to Katherine and bows again. "Ms. Mulwray, would you like to follow me?"

They retreat up the staircase to the second story.

When he's sure they're out of earshot, Hollis turns to his wife.

"Evelyn, for heaven's sake, what have you done?"

"What do you mean?"

"Well, won't she miss out on her exams if she leaves before the end of the semester?"

"Yes, but—"

"And what about her transcripts? Getting her into Stanford was going to be hard enough as it is. But now, if there are any gaps . . ."

"Darling, *please*. I had a call with her the other day, and she sounded so sad. I thought she could use a break."

"But the holidays are just a few months away." He pauses to take a big sip of his drink. "We were going to meet at Agua Caliente. I've already bought tickets."

Evelyn's about to respond when the butler approaches. He gives a curt nod as he passes by the living room on his way to the foyer. He gathers Katherine's luggage and returns, slowly, to the second floor.

"I don't know what the problem is, Hollis." Evelyn whispers since Khan is still on the stairs. "You're always saying how this house is too big for just the two of us. How we have so much space we don't know what to do with it."

Hollis sets down his cocktail and tries to patiently explain.

"Katherine was going to complete her studies in Mexico. You were both going to tour Europe for the summer and, after you returned, she was going to go to Stanford. Her coming to live with us was never part of the plan."

Evelyn shrugs, puts out the dying cigarette, and quickly lights another.

"Plans change."

He's about to speak when he hears footsteps on the stairs. It's the butler, returning for the rest of Katherine's things. He struggles with one of the trunks, barely managing it by himself. Hollis and Evelyn remain quiet until they hear Khan breathlessly drop the trunk on the landing of the second floor.

"But, Evelyn, do you think it's safe? What about . . ."

Hollis doesn't finish the sentence. He doesn't have to.

"There's nothing to worry about. My . . . father spends all his time on Catalina."

He knows this isn't true. Hollis has heard from various colleagues that Cross has lunch every Tuesday at the Pig 'n Whistle in Hollywood.

Evelyn reaches out and touches his shoulder, kneading his muscles through the light suit jacket.

"We could be a family, Hollis. Maybe she could even put off college for a year. I could get her a job in town. Something small, just to get her out of the house." She speaks slowly and softly, as if in a dream. "She'd make friends. We could buy her a car. She'd be a normal girl."

Hollis knows it's a bad idea but doesn't know what else to do.

"Okay, Evelyn. Whatever you say."

Hollis looks up from a stack of memos and correspondence to find Elwin Ransome standing in the door that opens onto the hallway. With one of his shirt tails hanging below his belt, Ransome's more disheveled than usual. Holding up a file folder filled with papers, he says, "It's not just the reservoirs."

"Are you sure?"

"I stayed late last night and pulled the drainage logs from every site in the basin. We're still seeing water loss across the board. But there's more."

"What?"

"Water's showing up where it shouldn't be."

"Where?"

Elwin approaches the desk and pulls a map from the file.

"The LA River, for starters. Under Hollenbeck Bridge."

He places the folder on the desk and unfolds a map of Los Angeles.

"These red circles show where we've had reports of unusual water dumping."

Hollis glances at the map. In addition to the LA River, he sees a circle around Point Fermin in San Pedro.

"How are we getting these reports?"

"Mostly just from the switchboard. I overheard a few of the girls yesterday talking in the lunchroom. Apparently, since we're in a drought and there's a heat wave, whenever there's water where there's not supposed to be water, people think there's something wrong and call it in."

Still examining the map, Hollis says, "Well, they're right. This is highly unusual."

Elwin turns to the folder. He opens it and flips through the papers, looking for something. Retrieving a sheet of lined paper covered in figures, he says, "Here's the latest on the reservoirs."

Something in the folder catches Hollis's eye. A heavy piece of paper folded in thirds. He remembers the threat that Elwin found earlier in the week, and Russ's subsequent question about the young engineer's character.

"What did you find?" Hollis finally asks.

"The numbers are worse than the other day. They're the lowest I've ever seen."

"This doesn't make any sense. To get the reservoirs down *this* low, there would have to have been some sort of official order."

Hollis turns and calls out to his secretary. A second later, she pokes her head into the office.

"Oramae, call Jack Tanner and see who authorized the drainage of any reservoirs in the past forty-eight hours."

She nods and retreats.

Turning back to the data, Hollis mutters, more to himself than to Elwin, "This doesn't make any sense. I could have sworn..."

His voice trails off as he pulls a memo from underneath a stack of letters.

"This is the daily report I get about water levels all over the county." Hollis runs a finger across the lines of numbers, comparing the figures he was given to what Elwin has compiled. "Each regional manager calls in and reports how much water they have on hand. All of those numbers are compiled into this memo."

Elwin cranes his neck so he can compare the numbers, too.

"They're different. The figures don't match up." Hollis

doesn't want to say what he's thinking, but he finally does. "Someone's filing false reports."

"Or calling in fake numbers," suggests Elwin. "But why?"

Hollis considers all of this.

"I'm not sure."

After a brief knock, the secretary enters the office, a perplexed look on her face.

"Did Tanner tell you who authorized the drainage?"

"Yes, Mr. Mulwray."

"Well, who was it?"

"He said it was you, sir."

Hollis calmly asks, "Can you repeat that?"

"He said *you* authorized it. He has a memo."

Hollis stands, grabs his hat, and begins to walk quickly out of the office.

Chasing after him, the secretary asks, "Where are you going, Mr. Mulwray?"

"I want to pay Jack Tanner a visit."

Tanner's office is just a floor below his, so Hollis takes the stairs. Elwin follows close behind.

Whereas Hollis's office has space for a conference table and chairs, bookshelves and display cases, all Tanner has space for is himself and a desk. He doesn't even have a secretary.

When Hollis enters the small space, Elwin stays behind in the hallway.

Tanner's seated, reading a report, an unlit cigar poking out of a corner of his mouth. A small electric fan on the cluttered desk rotates back and forth.

"Jack, what's this I hear about me authorizing drainage from the reservoirs?"

Tanner holds up a piece of paper.

"I got this the other day. You gave the order, and I relayed it to the district managers."

Hollis examines the memo. It's typed on his stationery. As Tanner looks on, puzzled, Hollis tries to figure out how this could have happened. He rarely locks his office, so almost anyone could have come in and taken a few pieces of stationery.

"Anything wrong, Hollis?"

He figures it's better to keep all this quiet until he can figure out for himself what's happening.

"No, nothing, Jack."

He thanks Tanner for his time and joins Elwin in the hallway.

"What happened?" Ransome asks. "What did he say?"

"He has a memo from me," Hollis sighs, "that I never sent."

"But what does that mean, Mr. Mulwray?" Elwin lowers his voice when two secretaries pass by. "Who would want to do such a thing?"

"I don't know, Elwin, but you keep digging. Whatever

you find, report back to me. And don't tell anyone else about this, okay? The reservoirs, the map, *nothing*. Not until I get to the bottom of it."

"Yes, Mr. Mulwray."

Hollis puts on his hat and walks toward the elevator.

"Where are you going?" Elwin calls out.

"LA River. I want to see the water for myself."

He drives out to Hollenbeck Bridge, cruising along its length before turning onto a sloping access road that leads down into the dry riverbed. The Buick kicks up dust as it descends, the ramp finally ending in a patch of gravel. Hollis stops the car and gets out. He can see, in a shady section under the bridge, a small pool of black water.

As he walks toward the water, sinking into the gravel with every step, he can feel the heat of the small stones through his shoes. Sand, for about ten yards in every direction, is moist and dark brown. The puddle, cloudy and oily, looks to be a few inches deep. Just beyond the water is a storm drain clogged with brush and rocks.

Next to the storm drain, leaning against one of the huge cement columns, is part of a billboard. The paint is cracked and faded, but the words are legible. OWN YOUR OWN OFFICE IN THIS BUILDING $5,000

TO $6,000. Hollis bends down and can see that the billboard forms the roof of a crude dwelling. Beside this is a battered chest of drawers. Scattered on the ground are various bits of men's clothing. A shoe, vest, two socks, a blue shirt drying on a stick. Hollis sniffs and smells ash coming from an oil drum.

He's about to pick up an Armour lard can when something moves inside the structure. A man crawls out wearing filthy pants and a wrinkled undershirt.

"Ahoy there."

"Well, hello." Hollis glances around, to see if anybody else is hiding in the shadows. "I'm not—I mean to say, I didn't expect to see anyone down here."

"I admit, as an address, it's off the beaten path." The man is weathered and old, his deeply tanned face making the white hair sticking out in all directions look even more white. "But you can't beat the rent."

The man walks to where the clothes sit on the gravel. He reaches for the shirt and begins to put it on.

"You live here?"

"That I do." Finished buttoning the shirt, he offers his hand. "Name's Leroy Shuhardt."

Hollis hesitates for a second before shaking the man's hand.

"Hollis Mulwray."

Leroy walks past the oil drum and plops down on a car seat. Hollis follows and sits on a wire milk crate. It's cool in the shade under the bridge. In the distance, the dry foothills are capped with power lines and an idle oil pump.

"Have you lived here long?"

"Few years." Leroy cocks his head back toward the city. "Before I came out here, I used to frequent Ferguson Alley."

"Chinatown?"

"That's right. The stretch between Los Angeles Plaza and Alameda Street." The old man's eyes shine when he speaks of it. "Used to get all types in Ferguson Alley. Sailors from Pedro, miners from up north. Cowboys, gamblers, gangsters. Never knew what was going to happen next. Saw more than one man beaten to death outside of the Kong Chow Temple. It was dangerous, but it was worth it. Back then, this city was an adventure."

"What is it now?"

Leroy grunts before answering.

"Business," he finally says.

"Is that why you came down here?"

"Not exactly. Whole area got bulldozed. It's now a freeway." He kicks at the moist ground, the dirt coming up in clumps. "I guess we all have to make way for the future. Whether we want to or not."

A truck passes by overhead, the engine backfiring.

"Do you mind if I ask you a few questions?" Hollis says.

"Ain't got nothing else to do."

"I work for the water department. We've had reports of water being dumped into the river over the past week. Have you seen anything like that?"

"Water? Sorry, that's not my liquid of choice." He produces from his hip pocket a pint of Old Forester whiskey. "Care to join me?"

Hollis smiles and waves away the man's offer.

"No, thank you."

Leroy takes a deep sip and wipes his mouth with the back of his hand.

"I might have heard something, but it's hard to tell with the cars overhead."

Hollis looks around.

"But there's water. And the sand is wet."

Leroy stares at the ground.

"Yes, sir, I guess it is."

"But you didn't see anything?"

The man laughs and waves the liquor bottle.

"I'm a very powerful sleeper."

Hollis looks around. None of this makes any sense.

"And it's just you out here?"

Leroy nods with his chin past the cement column, to where the gravel segues to larger rocks. Beyond this, green shrubs grow in the sand dunes and the dirt turns into a field.

"On the other side of the river there's a family of Mexicans. They might know something."

Hollis stands. All he sees is an old gray horse and a few structures even shabbier than Leroy's.

"Doesn't look like anyone's there."

"They usually go out during the day to look for work." Leroy takes another sip from the bottle. "Don't know if they ever find any."

"Well," Hollis says, "then maybe I'll come back. It was nice to meet you."

As he begins to walk away, the man calls after him.

"I don't understand."

Hollis stops and turns. Leroy speaks again.

"If you're from the water department, how come you don't know about the water?"

"It's a mistake. That's why I came here."

Leroy looks from Hollis to the mostly dry riverbed.

"If someone's trying to turn this back into a river, they have a long way to go. And I'm not even sure it'd be worth it."

"And why's that?"

"Like I said before, the future." He takes a final swig from the bottle. "There just ain't no going back to the way things were."

Hollis nods and says, "Good day."

Leroy calls after him again.

"Bring a bottle next time. Man's got to live on something more than just water!"

This time, Hollis doesn't turn around.

Back at the office, he puts in calls to the district managers. Each of them followed Tanner's orders based on the fake memo and proceeded to drain thousands of gallons of water from their reservoirs. Examining again Elwin's numbers from earlier in the morning, Hollis sees that Oak Pass Reservoir has experienced the biggest loss. It's only half of where it should be at this time of year.

Hollis gives the clock on his wall a quick glance. Quarter to five. He figures it's too late to get out to the reservoir today. He'll pay a visit after the weekend. On Monday, or maybe Tuesday after the hearing at city hall.

He's looking over the figures for a third time when his secretary enters with a stack of phone messages. He sees that Sam Bagby called twice.

Tossing the messages aside, he says, "Can you ask Russ to come see me?"

"I'm sorry, but Mr. Yelburton hasn't been in all day."

As she returns to her desk, Hollis walks to where the huge book of blueprints and surveys sits on the conference table. He examines the layout of the Oak Pass Reservoir, seeing where the channels lead. He grabs a pencil and a pad of paper and makes a few calculations of his own.

"I'm leaving for the night, Mr. Mulwray."

He looks up. His secretary is standing in the doorway, clutching her bag and wearing a light jacket.

"Good night, Oramae. I'll see you on Monday."

After she leaves, Hollis closes the big book. His head is swimming with numbers and theories, none of them adding up. Outside, in the hallway, more people head home for the weekend. Office doors open and close. Hollis hears muffled conversations, footsteps running for the elevator, laughter. Someone passing by loudly hums the melody to "I've Got You Under My Skin." Hollis thinks of Sadie and smiles.

He walks to his desk, picks up the phone, calls home. The butler answers.

"Good evening, Khan. It's Mr. Mulwray. I'm afraid I won't make it home for dinner again tonight."

Hollis waits for a response or some kind of acknowledgment, but there's just silence.

"Hello, Khan? Khan, are you there?"

After a few more seconds, there's a click and a new voice.

"Hollis, what's this I hear about you not coming home for dinner?"

"Well, hello, Evelyn, darling." He does his best to hide

his anger. "I didn't mean for Khan to bother you, but yes, I have another business engagement tonight."

"But what ... what about Katherine? She just got here. This is our first chance to have dinner as a family. The cook is making her favorite meal."

"It's just one night, Evelyn." He speaks calmly, not wanting to be drawn into a fight. "We have the whole weekend to be together."

"Yes, but she's looking forward to it. The table's already set for three, and I—"

"Now, Evelyn, if you'd have told me she was coming earlier in the week, I would have cleared my schedule. But *you* wanted to keep it a surprise, remember?"

In the silence, Hollis hears two sets of breath. Khan must be listening on the extension.

"Well, okay, but I want us to spend the entire weekend together. As a family."

"Thank you for understanding." He's about to hang up when he asks, "By the way, what is Katherine's favorite meal?"

There's more silence on the other line. Evelyn finally answers.

"Actually, I don't know. She spoke to the cook directly. Hollis, her Spanish really is good."

"I'll see you later tonight, darling."

"Goodbye, Hollis."

Even though it's early, because it's Friday, the Cocoanut Grove is already half-full. The maître d', recognizing Hollis from the previous night, seats him at the same table up front. The waitress also remembers him, and the large tip.

"Welcome back, sir, I'm so glad to see you. Can I start you off with another vodka daquiri?"

Hollis nods yes as he takes off his hat and sits down.

Waiting for his cocktail, he stares at the stage. In just a few minutes, Sadie will be standing there. He sniffs at the air, but what he gets is cigarette smoke. No lilacs.

The waitress drops off his drink. He takes a sip. It's growing on him.

Hollis scans the room. Women wear fancy dresses and glamorous makeup, and the men all have on dark suits despite the lingering summer heat. Looking at this crowd, you wouldn't know half the country's out of work.

"Why, Mr. Mulwray, two nights in a row?"

He turns and sees Sadie. She's wearing a deep-blue gown and large black costume jewelry made out of glass.

"I do believe this makes you a fan."

He stands and she plants a small kiss on each cheek. As she does, he takes a deep breath. Lilacs.

"Join me for a drink?"

"Well, maybe a small one."

She sits down and Hollis flags down the waitress. Sadie asks again for a whiskey and soda.

"I really enjoyed your show last night."

"You flatter me, Mr. Mulwray. I'm nothing special."

"Oh, I wouldn't say that."

A cigar girl walking by gives Sadie a funny look. Sadie ignores her.

"Are you still working on your case?"

"Case?" Hollis says. "Oh, the dam."

He nervously puts a hand in his pocket. He's still carrying around the buttons he found at Sadie's the day before.

"The truth is, I was thinking about you all day. I hope you don't mind I came again so soon."

"I'm glad you did. In fact, I have a favor to ask."

The waitress returns with the whiskey and Sadie takes a sip.

"My car's in the shop, so I was hoping you could stick around until after the show and give me a ride home."

Before answering, he takes a sip of his vodka. The cigar girl passes by again.

"Well, Sadie, I just don't know."

She places her hand on his.

"If it's too much to ask, I'll just take a cab."

"No," he says, removing his other hand from his pocket and placing it on top of hers. A large onyx ring presses against his soft palm. "I'd be honored to."

She smiles at him.

"Well then, consider it a date."

Hollis is about to say something when he stops, sensing a presence behind him. He turns, thinking it's the cigar girl.

"Hollis Mulwray, you're a hard man to get a hold of."

Sam Bagby stands with a group of men Hollis doesn't recognize. Sam is wearing a light wool suit and a big smile.

"Hope we didn't disturb anything."

Before Hollis can answer, Sadie gets up.

"Take my seat, please. I need to get going anyway. Show's about to start."

While Bagby watches Sadie walk away, Hollis stares down at the table. As Bagby approaches the table, he walks with a limp. He had polio as a child.

"I see you're enjoying the house specialty."

"Pardon?"

Sam points to Hollis's cocktail as he sits down.

"Oh, yes." Hollis picks up the glass and drinks the last few drops. "I've come to quite like them."

"I can see," Sam says, still smiling. He flags down the waitress. "Ida, bring us another round, will you? You know what I like, dollface."

"Right away, Mr. Bagby."

Turning back to Hollis, he says, "You've been avoiding me."

"I haven't been avoiding you. I've just been busy."

"You don't think I'm not busy, Hollis? Don't forget, I was mayor of this town for four years. That creates a lot of responsibilities, even now."

"Mayor," Hollis repeats. This makes him think of Jacob Hoke and the buttons. Bagby ran against Hoke in '29. "Sam, do you happen to know a man named Frank Starbard?"

Waving to someone in the crowd, Bagby says, distracted, "No, should I?"

"I don't know. He worked for that man you ran against, the Socialist. Jacob Hoke."

"What's that lousy red got to do with anything?"

"Probably nothing. But do you know where he is now? Did he stay in politics?"

Bagby shrugs.

"He bounced around for a while. Had a commune or something up north, then he was a lawyer. Last I heard he was a preacher at some hole in the wall downtown. Gives Sunday mass to the drunks."

"Do you happen to know which church?"

The waitress drops off their cocktails.

Sam lifts his martini, takes a sip, and says, "You finding religion?"

"No," Hollis replies, "just trying to find someone who worked for him."

Bagby leans back and calls out to one of his entourage.

"Petey, what's the name of the church where you told me you'd seen Hoke?"

The man steps forward.

"Trinity Methodist. Over on Towne."

"Thank you, Petey." Sam turns back to Hollis. "Now that I've given *you* a piece of information, I'd like you to return the favor."

"What do you want to know?"

"The city council meeting on Tuesday, the special hearing about the dam. Care to give me a sneak preview?"

"You know exactly what I'm going to say. It's what I've been saying all along. I'm not going to build it."

Bagby slams his fists on the table, spilling his martini.

"You're a fool, Mulwray. The hearing's a formality." He leans in close and whispers. "Do you think I'd take this all the way to the city council, or put up the bond issue, if I didn't already have the votes?"

Hollis doesn't reply. On the bandstand, the musicians begin taking their seats.

"I have some very powerful friends," Bagby continues. "Friends who used to be *your* friends. That reminds me, we never see you out at the club."

Hollis grabs his new drink as the band begins playing "Pennies from Heaven."

"I don't get out to Catalina much these days."

"Fishing's not your thing, I know." Bagby laughs.

Sadie takes the stage. After giving a small curtsy, she begins to sing.

"Every time it rains, it rains pennies from heaven."

"But then again," Bagby says, looking from Hollis to Sadie, "we all like to try new things."

Another of Bagby's men approaches and whispers something into his ear. Bagby nods twice and smiles. The man steps back and joins the others.

Pushing himself up from the table, Sam says, "We'd love to have you on our side on this, Mulwray."

"We?" Hollis repeats. "Who is 'we'?"

"You know who I mean." Once again, he looks from Hollis to the stage. "Be sure to tell that lovely wife of yours I said hello."

After watching Bagby limp away, followed by his entourage, Hollis focuses again on the stage. The spotlight on Sadie makes her positively glow. After the first song ends, the band quickly begins another. She closes her eyes and continues to sing.

"There's a rainbow on the river, the skies are clearing."

The waitress returns.

"And will you also be staying for dinner tonight?"

Hollis consider this. He considers everything.

Sadie's looking at him. It's like she's singing right to him.

"Yes. I'm staying."

On the drive to Sadie's house, she leans against him. He almost runs two red lights. Pulling up to the bungalow, he parks on the street, just like he did yesterday.

"See me in?"

Walking up the driveway, he looks at the broken cement. There's an oil stain, shiny underneath the porch light.

She opens the door. Music is playing. Jazz.

"Must have left the radio on." She grins. "I'm always doing that."

She enters the house. He falters for a second before following her in. The entryway is just shadows. The smell of stale cigarette smoke hangs in the air. He begins to walk toward the living room, but she takes his hand and leads him somewhere else.

Passing by the spare room, he sees the open closet where he'd found the buttons. The suits and shirts seem to be in a different arrangement from how he left them yesterday. He's trying to think about what this means when she pulls him into the bedroom. The smell is different here. Lilacs.

A glow from a radio in the corner provides the only light. The bed is unmade and the blue satin sheets, along with Sadie's gown, look almost black in the dark.

She turns to face him. The music on the radio is slow and dreamy. She's standing next to the bed, but he's still in the doorway.

"Mr. Mulwray, why are you all the way over there?"

Hollis walks toward her, removing his bow tie. She removes everything else.

Two hours later, he pulls up to his house. All the lights are out. The servants have gone home. Inside, Hollis pauses on the stairs. Not wanting to face Evelyn, he considers going into the backyard. He'd like to sit under the stars and stare into his tide pool. But he shakes off the thought and takes another step. Better get this over with.

At the end of the hallway, there's light underneath the door of the master bedroom. She's awake. Hollis takes a deep breath and enters the room.

Evelyn, wearing a pearl-colored silk nightgown, is in bed reading *Harper's Bazaar*. She says, looking up, "Hello, sweetheart, how was your evening?"

He mumbles "fine" and sits down on the bed next to her.

She sniffs at the air.

"Hollis, you smell like . . . cigarettes."

"The men I was with were smoking."

She doesn't look convinced, but she also doesn't question him further.

"Evelyn, I need to tell you something. It's about Noah."

"My f-father?"

"I'm afraid tonight I ran into someone who knows him. Sam Bagby."

"The old mayor?"

"They're pressuring me to build that new dam in Vallejo Canyon. He threatened to get your father involved."

She puts aside the magazine and sits up.

"What did he say?"

Hollis unties his bow tie for the second time that night.

"He didn't say much, exactly. Just insinuated."

"Insinuated what?"

"He mentioned the Albacore Club and said it'd be 'better for everyone' if I cooperated."

Noah Cross owns the club; it's where he and the business elite of Los Angeles gather to fish, socialize, and make deals. Everyone Hollis knows is a member.

Evelyn inches toward him and grabs his arm.

"Do you think he'll come here? What about Katherine?"

He can see the fear in her eyes.

"She shouldn't stay here," he says. "We need to move her."

Evelyn squeezes Hollis's arm so tightly her nails almost pierce the fabric of his sleeve.

"Move her where, Hollis?" she says in a panic.

As he considers this, a name flashes in his mind. Helmer Berry.

Hollis says, "I have an idea."

5

ON THE VERANDA, a dozen dishes crowd the glass tabletop. There are half-eaten pastries, a decanter of orange juice, a pot of coffee, a dish of scrambled eggs, bacon, sausage, and a stack of French toast nobody touched. Everybody's stuffed. Katherine now sits on the lawn near the tide pool, while Evelyn smokes a cigarette and Hollis finishes his coffee. Having promised to take Katherine riding after breakfast, Evelyn's wearing khaki jodhpurs, a cream-colored blouse, and brown boots. Hollis has on linen pants and a plaid sport coat over a striped shirt.

With a twig, Katherine begins making eddies in the tide pool. She's dressed in borrowed riding clothes, from Evelyn, that are too large and don't fit.

Evelyn places a hand on her husband's shoulder and whispers, "Does she really have to leave?"

"You know your father, darling."

At the mention of Cross, Evelyn tenses up and pulls her hand away.

"I wish there was another way, Evelyn, but it's not worth taking a chance. You know what he's like."

Katherine looks their way and smiles. Hollis waves and smiles back.

Among all the things she's been told over the years, he wonders if Evelyn's ever told Katherine the truth. She must have wondered why they're not like other families, why they've spent so little time together. Or maybe, to her, all of this is normal. She doesn't know anything different.

"What will you tell him?"

Shaken from this thought, Hollis asks, "Who?"

"The man at the apartments. El Dorado, or whatever it's called. That place you told me about."

"The manager? If I pay for six months in advance, I don't think he'll ask too many questions."

The sun is now directly over the backyard. Evelyn puts out her cigarette and shields her eyes.

"In fact," Hollis continues, "maybe I'll pay with a

departmental check. That way I can say it's for someone who's in from out of town. A specialist or something. An engineer."

"But why not just pay with cash, or a personal check?"

Servants emerge from the house and, squinting, begin to retrieve the plates and dishes. Hollis waits for them to leave before speaking again.

"Cash would be suspicious—a middle-aged man paying rent for a young girl—and your father knows too many people at the bank."

When Evelyn grabs for another cigarette, her hands are shaking.

"Evelyn, it will be okay, trust me. You two go for your ride and I'll take care of everything. When I get back, we'll help her pack and take her over."

Evelyn, blowing out smoke, reluctantly nods. The servants gather the last of the dishes. All that remains on the table are the half-filled glasses.

Katherine, sensing a break in their conversation, looks up from the tide pool.

"Papa, will you teach me what some of these animals are?"

"Later, sweetheart." He waves her over. "We have something to tell you first."

She rises from the lawn and wipes the grass from the seat of her pants.

"What is it?"

Evelyn looks at Hollis. Hollis looks at Katherine. Her eyes are impossibly blue.

"You know what? Let's save all of that for later."

"Are you sure, Papa?"

"Yes, darling. Now go inside and get washed up for your ride."

Katherine smiles and runs inside the house. Evelyn gets up and kisses him on the cheek.

"Thank you, Hollis."

After she enters the house, he calls after her, "Promise me you'll use a saddle. I don't want to hear about any of this nonsense of riding bareback."

To himself, taking the last sip of cold coffee, he says, "Damn woman is going to get herself killed."

At the office main lobby, Hollis doesn't recognize the guard on duty, an older man with silver hair. The guard seems to know him.

"Putting in a few extra hours, Mr. Mulwray?"

Hollis just grins and tips his straw Panama hat as he strides toward the elevators. Walking to his office on the sixth floor, Hollis hears something. Footsteps, papers shuffling. Looking through the frosted glass of the door in the hallway, he sees a shadowy figure. Someone's inside his office.

He briefly considers going downstairs to get the guard before deciding to handle this himself. Hollis takes a deep breath and opens the door.

Elwin, standing in front of the conference table, jumps. He has a pencil in one hand and a piece of paper covered in numbers in the other. The big book of blueprints and maps is open to a different page than it had been the day before.

"Ransome, my God, you scared me half to death."

"Sorry, Mr. Mulwray." He points to where Hollis is, half inside the office and half in the hallway. "The door wasn't locked."

"That's because I didn't lock it. I never do." Hollis enters the office and closes the door behind him. "What are you doing here?"

Elwin points to the open book.

"I'm just—I wanted to compare some channel measurements to ones that I had downstairs. To make sure that mine weren't off."

"And that couldn't wait until Monday?"

Elwin doesn't answer. He just continues to stare, his eyes open wide.

As Hollis approaches, he notices that Elwin's wearing a navy-blue yachting jacket, white trousers, and a straw fedora hat.

"Why are you dressed like that?"

"Like what?"

"Like a yachtsman."

"Well, Mr. Yelburton invited me to his club this afternoon."

Hollis walks to his desk and looks it over, to see if anything's missing. Or has been added—he remembers the heavy white paper folded in thirds he saw the day before in Elwin's folder.

"When did he do that?"

"Yesterday."

"I didn't think Russ was in the office at all yesterday. My secretary said—"

Elwin, his face flushing a dark red, cuts him off. "He called me at home. Last night."

"Is it normal for Mr. Yelburton to call you at home on a Friday night?"

"I don't know if it's normal for Mr. Yelburton. It certainly wasn't normal for me."

"What did he want?"

Hollis inspects the various piles of letters and memos. Everything seems to be the way he left it.

"To invite me to his club today, like I said. On Catalina."

"Albacore?"

Elwin's face brightens at the name.

"You know it?"

"My father-in-law owns it."

"Then you must go there all the time."

"I'm afraid that I don't." Hollis walks back to the conference table. "How did this come up?"

"I was in his office the other day, and I was remarking upon all his fishing stuff."

Yelburton has a number of pictures and decorations in his office. A mounted marlin, a photo of him posing with a large tuna, a small Albacore Club flag.

"And?"

"And, well, I asked him if he was the one who caught those fish, and he said he was. Then he said I should come out sometime."

"When was this?"

"The other day. I'd come by to see you, but your secretary said you were in the field. Mr. Yelburton heard me in the foyer and called me in."

"Did you tell Russ what you had intended to tell me?"

Elwin, looking a bit nervous, nods his head, yes.

"You told him about the reservoirs? And the river?"

"Just the reservoirs. I hadn't heard about the river yet."

"And what did Mr. Yelburton say?"

The young engineer shrugs.

"He didn't say much of anything, if I remember. He just started talking about fish. And then the club."

"I thought you said *you* were the one who brought up the fish?"

"Did I?"

Before Elwin can say anything else, the phone rings. The sound echoes throughout the quiet floor. Hollis lets it ring.

"Are—aren't you going to answer that?"

After two more rings, Hollis finally picks it up.

"Hello?" There's just silence. "Who is this?"

Breathing and faint noises. Footsteps, whispers. The line goes dead.

Hollis puts the phone down and says to the engineer, "I think you should go now, Elwin."

"Mr. Mulwray, please. Let me explain."

"Goodbye, Elwin."

After Ransome slinks out of the office, Hollis hears the elevator doors open and close.

Rattled by the encounter with Elwin, Hollis momentarily forgets what he came to the office for. Then it comes back to him. The checkbook, Katherine. The apartment.

He sits down at his desk and begins opening and closing drawers, looking for the checks. He finds various items. Keys, grooming kit, a menu from a lunch in 1913 at the Biltmore hotel. He takes out the menu and grins.

It was a party thrown by the water department to celebrate the opening of the Navarro valley aqueduct. Many bottles of champagne were consumed, and the whole room got rather tipsy and loud. Hollis chuckles, remembering the red-faced manager who'd come to complain to

Cross. Noah later took Hollis aside and told him that if he played his cards right, he could be chief engineer one day. It seemed at the time like idle conversation, drunken chatter meant to be forgotten. Hollis was just a kid at the time. But it somehow came true.

He puts the menu back and continues to search. In the top drawer he finds the checkbook. Westland National Bank. He rips off a check and puts it into his coat pocket.

Downstairs, he's passing by the front desk when he abruptly stops. The guard snaps to attention. Hollis says, "That man who just left."

"The skipper?" The guard laughs. "What about him?"

"How long was he in the building for?"

"About an hour, I suppose. They both were."

Hollis nods and takes a step before stopping.

"Both?"

The guard nods.

"There was another fella with him."

"Did the other man leave before him?"

"No, they left together. Just a few minutes before you came down. Arrived together, too."

"What did this other man look like?"

The guard laughs again and shakes his head.

"Not like you water department guys, I'll tell you that. He was big and dumb-looking, with a short tie and cigar. Smelled of gin and didn't say much."

Casting his mind back to earlier in the week, Hollis

remembers the man Russ introduced him to, the one who was going to guard the reservoirs.

"Mulvihill?"

"Can't say since neither introduced themselves."

"Well, thank you, you've been helpful."

The man nods and says, "You have a good rest of your weekend, Mr. Mulwray."

At the El Macando, the FOR RENT sign is still placed in the middle of the lawn. Hollis walks quickly past the row of brass mailboxes on his way to the manager's apartment. He gives the door two loud knocks with his fist.

The same man from the other day answers, only his hair's messier and there are soup stains on the once-white undershirt. Behind him, Hollis sees the keys hanging on the nail.

"Back again, eh? You want the apartment, or more information?"

"The apartment, actually." Hollis clears his throat and launches into the explanation he'd concocted on the drive over. "You see, we have a young woman from back east. An engineer. Student, that is. An engineering student. An intern, sort of. She'll be needing a place to stay for a few months."

"Young woman?" the manager repeats. "Student? I bet."

Hollis ignores this.

"It's also a bit of a last-minute situation, I'm afraid. My secretary got the dates mixed up and she's coming in on the 20th Century Limited tonight. Would it be a problem for her to move in right away?"

The manager grins. He's enjoying this.

"Sure, sure," he laughs. "As long as you pay the rent, your little cookie can do whatever she wants."

Hollis takes out the check.

"She may be here for a while. Can I pay six months, in advance?"

The manager's eyes light up.

"For six month's rent, my friend, I'll move her in myself."

Hollis writes the check. Handing over the slip of paper, he says, "I added on a little something extra, for the inconvenience."

The manager takes the check, licks his lips, and reaches for the key. It's attached to a cheap tin key chain that's a palm tree with a 12 at the center.

"I'll show you the way."

Hollis takes the key.

"I can find it myself, thank you."

He turns and walks toward the other side of the complex. The building is much quieter than it was the other day. He doesn't hear any conversations or radios. No crying, no fights. Hollis figures, because it's a Saturday afternoon and the day is cool, with an ocean breeze, everyone's gone out to enjoy the respite from the recent heat.

He finds number 12 and lets himself in.

It's a nice-sized one-bedroom apartment. Small couch, table and chairs, kitchen with a black-and-white tile floor. He sees a coffeepot, toaster, and a small refrigerator. Opening up the cabinets, he finds mismatched plates and dishes. In the drawer there's an assortment of silverware. The unit must have been vacant for a while. Everything has a layer of dust.

A door off the kitchen opens onto a private inner courtyard that contains a cheap iron table and chairs. The space is long and narrow, but also shaded. Looking up, Hollis can see the red Spanish tiles of the building next door.

He goes back into the apartment. The bedroom has a twin bed and a small dresser. The walls are decorated simply and anonymously, with cheap paintings of the beach and sea. In the bathroom, coral-colored towels hang from hooks.

Katherine, he hopes, will be happy here. And safe.

He exits the apartment, locks the door, and walks back to the Buick.

A few blocks from the apartment building, Hollis realizes he's being followed. A blue Ford coupe has been trailing him since he turned onto Franklin. At first he thought it was a coincidence. The car behind him was only by chance taking the same turns and streets as Hollis. But after two detours and a number of random turns and lane changes, with the Ford remaining close behind him every time, there's no doubt.

Hollis can see in the rearview mirror that it's a man. He can't see much more than that because a dark fedora is pushed down low. All Hollis can see of his face is a square jaw and a lit cigarette.

Hollis begins to go slow on Los Feliz Boulevard, trying to plan his next move. Confronting Elwin in his office was simple enough, but the idea of confronting whoever's in the Ford feels far riskier. Stopped behind a light at Hobart, Hollis makes a decision. He's got to lose the other car. As the light turns green, Hollis floors it.

The Buick, its engine roaring and the car rocking from side to side, picks up so much speed Hollis barely makes the turn onto Fern Dell Drive, heading into the hills. He looks hopefully to the rearview mirror. The Ford is still behind him, the cigarette now clenched between teeth.

Hollis begins to panic. If the car hits him—and Hollis

is forced to get out—he'd prefer that happen where there are witnesses. But as he careens down the winding, residential streets, he doesn't see a single person. He doesn't even see any homes. They're all hidden by hedges or a line of trees. Occasionally he spots a garage or a front door placed far behind a set of iron gates, but otherwise there's no one around.

After hurtling down two short streets that are just wide enough for the Buick, he makes a hairpin turn. The tires barely grip the pavement. Beyond a trio of garbage cans, Hollis spots an open garage. He slams on the brakes and somehow maneuvers the Buick inside, managing to not slam into the back wall. He jumps out of the car and lunges for the garage door. He closes it just as the Ford turns the corner and drives by. Through a series of glass panels in the door, Hollis watches the car pass.

He continues to watch the street from the garage, getting his breath back and making sure the Ford doesn't return. Turning back to his car he can see, through a gap in a door at the back wall, a long set of steps leading down to the home the garage belongs to. The long, rectangle-shaped house is built into the hill and has an expansive view of the city.

Convinced the car isn't returning, Hollis pushes up the garage door and carefully backs out the Buick.

To make sure he's not followed he takes the long way home, driving through Hollywood and wending around the canyons before approaching the city from the valley, like how he drove back from the dam the other day. It takes so long it's almost dark by the time he finally pulls into the driveway.

Entering the house, Hollis sees the trunks and matching luggage stacked in front of the coat closet. The monogram etched into the chrome shines dully in the half-light. KAM. He can hear Katherine, upstairs, crying. Evelyn must have told her.

SUNDAY MORNING IS nothing like Saturday morning. Neither of them has much of an appetite, most of the food the servants prepare goes untouched, and it's foggy and cold so they're at the dining room table and not outside. Instead of eating, Evelyn repeatedly stabs at half a grapefruit while Hollis only has coffee and reads the newspapers.

The night before, after dinner at a small Italian restaurant on Melrose, they drove Katherine to the apartment. Khan met them there, with the trunks and luggage in the back of a cousin's truck. Katherine actually seemed excited. She smiled and talked about it as being an adventure. Living on her own in the Big City. "It's like a movie," she kept saying. Evelyn, who'd had too much to drink at dinner, wept silently and had to be helped to the car by Hollis as they left. She didn't say anything on the drive home. Neither did he. Hollis was watching for the Ford that had followed him earlier in the day.

"I hope Katherine is okay."

Looking from the newspaper to his wife, Hollis says, "I'm sure she's doing fine, darling."

"We shouldn't have taken her there. She'll be lonely."

"We had to, Evelyn. You know that." Hollis turns a page. "This is what's best for everyone, especially her."

Evelyn trades the grapefruit for a pack of Lucky Strikes. She lights one and inhales deeply.

"After I go water Violet's plants out at Santa Monica, I'm going to go see Katherine. Take her some groceries."

He finishes with one section of the paper and begins another.

"I think that's a good idea."

"She's been learning to cook. She wants to have us over."

"Of course. Anytime."

One of the servants comes in with yet another plate of food. Evelyn just waves it away without even looking at it.

"I suppose I can talk to Natalie at I. Magnin," she says.

"Maybe they can take her on as a salesgirl. Even if she only earns commission, it'll be spending money."

Hollis flips down a corner of the paper.

"This is what you wanted, isn't it? For Katherine to feel like a normal girl? Get a job, an apartment, start living her life?"

"I know," Evelyn says. "I just wish we'd had more time together as a family."

Hollis stops reading and considers this. Had they ever been a family? Was that even possible given the circumstances? He'd tried to do things a father would do. One Christmas he taught Katherine to ride a bike, and during a summer trip he showed her how to swing a tennis racquet. But it always felt false, like they were only pretending. He sometimes wondered if any good could be made out of the ugliness that had happened. He turns his attention back to the paper.

Evelyn peers through the French doors and says, "It's so gray out."

Hollis puts down the *Examiner* and reaches for the *Post-Record*.

"It'll clear up. It always does."

"Do you want to go with me?" She stubs out the cigarette. "To the store and then to see Katherine?"

"No," he says, "I have to run an errand. Downtown."

She nods at this and leaves the table.

A servant, the young Mexican girl, comes to clear

some of the plates and dishes. Once again, she refuses to make eye contact.

Hollis holds up his nearly empty cup.

"Mas café, por favor."

"Sí, señor."

After the girl retreats to the kitchen, Hollis yawns. He didn't sleep much the night before. He had the dream again. The rushing water, the black wave, death.

Putting his hand in his pocket, he feels the buttons he took from the closet at Sadie's.

Hollis knows it's a long shot to see if Jacob Hoke remembers Frank Starbard, but since he can't connect the name *Essie* to anything, it's the only information he has. The city council meeting is on Tuesday and the bond issue is following shortly after. If he's going to stop the new dam, and put an end to his nightmares, he'd better come up with some answers, fast.

The girl comes back with the pot of coffee. Steam flows out of the fluted silver spout. When she pours the black liquid into the ornate china cup, she smiles. Her teeth are as white as bone.

Hollis feels self-conscious parking the polished Buick in front of the run-down church, but he doesn't have much of a choice. The whole block is a mess. Windows are smashed, men are passed out on the garbage-strewn sidewalk, and hungry kids peek out from alleys looking more like wild animals than children. He'd considered leaving the car a few streets away—in a nicer part of town—and approaching the church on foot, but Skid Row stretches so far in every direction he'd be walking for miles. Hoping for the best, Hollis gets out of his car and enters the building.

The church, the same as every other structure up and down Towne Avenue, is old and dilapidated. The European tradition of stained glass and Gothic design is nowhere to be seen here. Instead, cheaply printed posters with Bible verses are hung on dirty walls along with flyers announcing a schedule of free meals. In the corner there's a fountain with a small trickle of water, but Hollis isn't sure if it's for drinking or holy water used for services.

The chapel is just a big rectangular space with a high ceiling. On the wall are more posters, edges curled and hung crooked. The wooden pews are all askew. Hollis suspects men sleep on the floor at night. The altar is simple, with minimal decoration or religious totems—it looks more like a workbench than an altar. A large plaster crucifix is attached to the back wall, the only real religious decoration in the room.

Hollis had meant to time his visit to coincide with the end of services, arriving just as the faithful were leaving. He figured this would give him a chance to catch Hoke alone. But he's misjudged his entrance. The room is almost completely filled, and a minister with a deep voice is addressing the parishioners. Hollis tries to be inconspicuous as he takes a seat toward the back.

On the floor, in front of the altar, rests a big steel tub filled with water. It looks like something animals would drink out of on a farm. A fat man in an undershirt sits in the water. Dark pants can be seen under the still surface. Hanging from a candlestick on the altar is the man's shirt and brown coat. The minister, wearing a black suit, kneels beside the man in the tub. Hollis recognizes the minister as Jacob Hoke.

He remembers seeing Hoke's picture in the paper and on posters when he ran for mayor. Back then his hair was black and long in the front, always splayed over his large forehead. Now his hair is gray and thin, and his face is gaunt and weathered.

The fat man in the tub is sideways to Hoke and, as the minister speaks, both he and the man in the tub close their eyes.

"Do you repent of your sins and acknowledge your need of a Savior?"

Hoke's words echo in the huge room.

The man replies, quietly, "I do."

Leaning forward and placing one hand on the man's

back and the other on his chest, Hoke says, "Have you put your faith in Jesus as your Lord and Savior?"

"I have."

Looking down the row of pews, Hollis sees nothing but dirty necks and rags. This is the first church he's been in that smells of sweat rather than incense.

"Do you believe that he died and was raised to life?"

The man in the tub, beginning to sob, says again, "I do."

"Then in obedience to our Lord and Savior Jesus Christ, and upon your profession of faith, I baptize you, my brother, in the name of the Father, Son, and Holy Spirit. Amen."

As Hoke places both arms around the man's shoulders and slowly guides him backward into the water, the man reaches up with his right hand to plug his nose. As he becomes completely submerged, the crowd rises to their feet, as if this were a magic trick and the fat man might disappear under the small waves. After a few seconds, Hoke pulls the man up and gives him a long embrace. They both stand, the fat man smiling beatifically as he drips onto the floor. The front of Hoke's black suit is similarly soaked.

Raising his hands to the parishioners, Hoke announces, "The grace of our Lord Jesus Christ be with your spirit, brothers and sisters. Thank you for coming, and amen."

The crowd amen in unison and then begin to slowly file out of the church. Hoke hands the soaked man a towel as well as his shirt and jacket. The man walks toward the foyer, his hair still wet and the smile still on his face. His bare feet leave ghostly imprints on the cement floor.

Hoke turns and begins to gather the few things on the altar as the final parishioners exit. When the room is empty, Hollis clears his throat loudly. The minister turns and notices him sitting in a pew.

"How can I help you, brother?"

"My name is Hollis Mulwray. I'd like to ask you some questions."

Hoke squints as he assesses the stranger in his church.

"Yes, I believe I've heard of you. Water department, correct?"

Hollis nods, impressed.

"Tell me, do you work for Noah Cross? I had many a run-in with him back in the day."

"He retired some years ago. I'm in charge now."

Hoke steps down off the altar and sits in a pew across from Hollis.

"Well then, what can I help you with?"

"Do you remember the Van der Lip Dam? The disaster?"

"Yes. Five hundred innocent souls were lost. Terrible tragedy."

"Well, I'm looking for a man who might have some information about the dam. About the day it failed. Frank Starbard. I believe he worked on your campaign in '29."

Hoke closes his eyes and nods slowly.

"We came pretty close. Received 44 percent of the vote. Forced a runoff."

"You likely would have won," Hollis says, "if it weren't for the trial."

Hoke had thrown his support behind two brothers accused of bombing a newspaper. The pair had professed their innocence since the beginning, claiming to be the victims of anti-worker persecution. Celebrated lawyer Henry Drummond was defending them but, on the eve of the election, they changed their pleas to guilty. Support for Hoke and the Socialist Party collapsed overnight.

"That was a long time ago," Hoke finally says, opening his eyes.

"Do you remember Starbard?"

"I believe so. Tall, dark hair, strong."

Hollis nods and says, "What did he do for the campaign?"

"Not much of anything, now that I remember. Was in charge of a branch of our volunteers. Knocking on doors, handing out pamphlets, that kind of thing. Frank, as I recall, was only interested in young female volunteers."

"He wasn't a true believer?"

"I didn't try to look into either his mind or his heart. We needed a lot of help at the time, and he helped—in his own way."

"Have you heard from Starbard since the election, or more recently?"

"No. Once the results from the runoff came in, and it turned out we lost, I never heard from him again."

"I understand you got out of politics."

Hoke nods.

"Bought some land and moved out to Antelope Valley. Two thousand acres. Started with just five families but, in a few years, we'd built a community of nearly a thousand. We had a sawmill, restaurants, a school. It was a true cooperative. Even had our own newspaper. It was a glorious thing."

Hollis remembers hearing of the colony, but only as a source of ridicule. All the local papers, especially the *Times,* had a field day printing and relishing every setback the community encountered.

"I don't believe I ever heard what happened. Does it still exist?"

Hoke laughs darkly.

"No, Mr. Mulwray. We had to abandon the colony some years ago."

"Why?"

"Water. Without water we just couldn't make it work.

The land had included water rights—we'd made sure of that—but as we began to grow, some farmers nearby claimed we were using too much. We petitioned the state to allow us to build a dam but were turned down. 'Your people do not seem to have the necessary amount of experience or money it will involve.' Money," he laughs, "it always comes down to money."

"Well, Mr. Hoke, I can tell you that dams are indeed expensive. And building one does take a lot of experience."

The minister cocks his head and says, "What about your dam, Mr. Mulwray, the one that failed? Didn't Noah Cross have money and experience?"

There's nothing Hollis can say to this, so he just stares at the floor.

"Mr. Mulwray, our whole experiment existed to solve the problem of unemployment, and now look at us. Not only Los Angeles, but the country. People can't get work for love or money. So you tell me who's right and who's wrong."

"I don't know about any of that, Mr. Hoke. I'm just in charge of the water."

"Water is power, Mr. Mulwray. You must realize that by now. It's a weapon." The minister's voice rises and fills the empty chapel. "Water can kill the same as a gun or a knife. The lack of it killed my colony, and that fracture at the dam killed those poor people who lived in its path."

Hollis smiles. He can see how Hoke almost became mayor.

"You know, whether it was my colony or my career in politics, all I ever tried to do was one thing: lift people out of poverty." He stops and shrugs. "But maybe that's just something that's not going to be allowed to happen. Even Jesus says this: 'Every culture will have poor people because of the nature of this world.' And going against the nature of this world is not something I'd advise you to do."

"I don't believe I follow what you're saying."

"Sometimes what you're trying to cure can't be cured. Or what you think is broken is just the way the thing's meant to be." He stops and looks up to the ceiling before continuing. "And sometimes the mystery you're trying to solve, Mr. Mulwray, is no mystery at all."

Hollis gives a small laugh and stands up.

"Thank you for your time, Mr. Hoke."

As Hollis begins to walk away, Hoke gets up and calls after him.

"The dam, Mr. Mulwray. The one that failed. How did you come to build it where it was?"

Hollis stops and turns. He thinks back.

"Well, I wasn't chief engineer back then. It wasn't my decision. However, as you might imagine, a lot of factors go into choosing a site. There's the soil, the surrounding—"

"No." Hoke shakes his head, cutting off Hollis. "I don't mean all that. What I'm asking you to consider is why was it built there. Out of all the locations it could have had."

Hollis grins.

"Are you alluding to an unseen force, or some other kind of power? Fate, maybe? Something that can't be controlled, or stopped?"

Hoke smiles and says, "You know, it's funny. I started my career as a lawyer, and it seems to me I'm ending it as a minister. In both you're serving something you can't always see. First it was justice, and now it's God."

Hollis puts his hands in his pockets and says slowly, "I'm sorry, Mr. Hoke, but I don't think I believe in either."

"You don't have to, Mr. Mulwray. These things believe in you, and that's enough."

Back on the street, Hollis is pleased to see that the Buick is still there and in one piece. However, a small crowd has gathered. Three kids stand on the running board, peering inside, while a man with hollowed-out eyes runs his hands along the gleaming hood. Hollis shoos them away and gets into the car.

He drives down Towne and makes a right onto Fifth.

Stopped behind a light, he watches as a blue Ford coupe passes through the intersection, heading north. Hollis turns just in time to see blue pinstripes and a trail of cigarette smoke. A chill goes down his spine. The light turns green and someone has to honk to get Hollis to move. He quickly makes a right turn and begins to follow the Ford.

The coupe is a few car lengths ahead, but Hollis is pretty sure it's the car from the day before. The man's shoulders, the fedora, the suit and cigarette—it's all the same.

Hollis wonders what he should do. Get closer? Force the car off the road? If he did either of those things, what would happen next? He looks at the license plate: 62 S 895. The combination of letters and numbers means nothing to him, but he memorizes it anyway. Tomorrow he could call his friend at the Highway Patrol, and maybe that would get him the driver's address. However, tomorrow might be too late.

Hollis is now right behind the blue coupe. The Ford makes a left turn and Hollis does the same.

After a few blocks, Hollis begins to feel sick when he realizes he's on West Fourth. This is Sadie's street. He quickly reasons this away, thinking it's just a coincidence. The street probably means nothing. Los Angeles is full of them. But when the Ford passes Plymouth, and begins to slow down, he can no longer deny it.

Hollis watches as the Ford pulls into the driveway of

the bungalow. He quickly pulls to the side of the road and parks. He has a good view as the driver gets out of the car, fedora in hand. It's the man in the photo on the mantel, Frank Starbard. Sadie's husband. Hollis hears the front door of the bungalow open and slam closed.

7

"Tell me that again."

Elwin is standing in front of Hollis's desk. He has the same file folder as the other day, only now it contains just one piece of paper. He repeats, "I was wrong."

"You were wrong about what?"

He pulls out the sheet of figures and hands it to Hollis.

"The reservoirs. The river, everything. The levels in the reports, they're correct. I must have made a mistake."

Hollis looks over the numbers. He compares them to the official report that he found on his desk that morning. The numbers, every one of them, match. He looks from the paper to Elwin. The young engineer's face and neck are a shade of reddish orange they weren't the other day.

"Looks like you got a sunburn over the weekend."

"I went to Catalina, remember?"

"I remember." Hollis crumples the sheet of figures into a ball and tosses it into the trash. "Did he pay you, Elwin?"

"Who?"

"Yelburton. Did he give you money in exchange for changing your reports? For lying about the levels?"

"No, Mr. Mulwray. It's nothing like that."

"Then who was it?"

Considering all the rich and powerful men who gather at the Albacore Club, and knowing the millions that are at stake, there would have been numerous parties interested in corrupting the young engineer.

"It was nobody."

"Then I don't understand how the numbers you showed me last week suddenly went away. I don't know how all of that water magically returned."

Elwin puts his head down and speaks into his chest.

"I told you, I was mistaken."

Hollis slaps at his desk. The photo of Evelyn falls over.

"I went out there, Elwin. To the river. I saw the water. Why are you denying it?"

The young engineer doesn't speak. The phone on Hollis's desk rings, and he hears his secretary in the next room answer it. He pauses for a second, seeing if Oramae will buzz him on the intercom to say it's Yelburton. Russ had left a message earlier saying he had to check out something in the valley, but that he would call in if he could.

"Then what was it," Hollis continues, "a promotion? Did he say you could be a regional manager, or did he do something really foolish, like promise you Tanner's job?"

His head still down, Elwin squeaks, "I don't know what you're talking about."

Exasperated, Hollis places both hands on his desk and says slowly, "Ransome, you're fired. Get out."

Elwin looks up quickly. His reddened face somehow gets even redder.

"You can't do that."

"Can't I? I'm chief engineer. If you're not out of the building in ten minutes, I'm going to call security."

Elwin slinks out of the office and slams the door behind him. A second later, Hollis's secretary peeks her head into the room.

"Mr. Mulwray, is everything okay?"

"No, it's not, Oramae. I just fired Elwin Ransome. Notify Personnel, and then call Jack Tanner. Tell him to revoke Ransome's clearance and make sure he alerts the regional managers. I think he and Russ are up to something."

She looks worried but nods and says, "Yes, Mr. Mulwray."

"I need to prepare for the city council meeting tomorrow, so please hold all my calls. I don't want to be disturbed."

She nods again and closes the door. Hollis pulls out from a mound of paperwork the independent assessment of the Alto Vallejo Dam that had been prepared by the American Society of Civil Engineers. He flips through the pages, refreshing his memory. It's been months since he looked at the plans. He takes a piece of department stationery and makes some notes. *112 ft. high. Slopes of 2½ to 1. Dirt banked. 12,000-acre water surface.* He sighs. It's Van der Lip all over again.

As he's turning to a table of charts in the back of the report, his phone rings. He hears his secretary answer it in the other room. A second later there's a knock at his door.

"Goddamn, Oramae, I asked not to be disturbed."

"I'm sorry, Mr. Mulwray, but it's the police. He says it's an emergency."

Hollis drops his pencil and grabs at the black receiver.

"Mr. Mulwray? This is Detective Holabird from the LAPD. We met the other day. Listen, I'm at a house in Downey and we'd like you to come by. Can I give you the address?"

"Is this about the letters? Do you know who sent them?"

"I'm afraid I can't discuss it over the phone."

"Detective, I'm a very busy man. You must tell me what this is regarding. Tomorrow I have to be at city hall for a—"

"Just get out here. I'd like you to identify a dead body."

The small yellow house sits on a quiet side street. Hollis doesn't need to check the address, he just parks near the police cars. Getting out of the Buick, he searches his memory, trying to think back. Does he know who lives here? Has he ever been on this street? He comes up blank on both questions.

The front door is open, and uniformed officers walk in and out. No one stops Hollis or asks him what he's doing there. In the kitchen, a number of men are drinking coffee from paper cups. One of them calls out to him.

"Mr. Mulwray, thank you for coming."

It's the detective from last week, Wallace Holabird. The other men, presumably detectives—they're all dressed in the same kind of cheap summer suit—exit the house.

"Would you please follow me?"

The detective leads him to a bedroom. It looks like any other bedroom. There's a nightstand, lamp, drapes, open closet, unmade bed. On the floor is a man in a robe. His face has been almost completely shot away. The only thing that remains is one ear and some hair. The rest of his head is on the wall and baseboard. A large revolver is a few feet from the body. Hollis has to press a handkerchief to his mouth to stop from gagging.

"I don't suppose you know this man," the detective says. "Or, rather, that you *knew* him."

Hollis bends down slightly to get a closer look. The pooled blood on the carpet is black. Flies buzz around it.

"I don't know . . . or rather, I can't tell who it is."

"Well then, maybe you can tell me why he was in possession of this."

The detective holds out something and Hollis takes it. It's one of the detective's business cards. On the back is Hollis's name and phone number.

"Oh my God."

"You know who it is?"

"Yes. His name is Elmer Fowler."

"How do you know him?"

Hollis shrugs.

"I don't, really."

"Mr. Mulwray, don't get cute. The man has my card with your name on it. I gave you the card a week ago today, and now this man is dead. I want to know why."

"I'd gone to see him. At a movie set. I didn't have anything to write on except your card, so I gave him that and told him to call me if he thought of anything else."

"Did he?"

"No, I never heard from him again."

After a brief knock at the door, a man enters with a black satchel and a camera on a leather strap around his neck.

"Hiya, Harvey," the detective says, stepping aside. "Take pictures and look for fingerprints, will ya?"

The man with the camera nods and places the satchel on the floor. As he begins to pull out various bits of equipment, the detective and Hollis walk back to the living room.

"So, what was he, an actor?"

"Not exactly," says Hollis. "He was just an extra."

"And what had you gone to see him about? The notes?"

"No. It was about the dam. He was a highway patrolman, years ago. He'd stopped a car the night the dam broke. I went to see if he could remember anything else about it."

"And did he?"

"Sort of." Hollis shrugs. "He gave me a name—Essie—but I haven't been able to find anyone who matches it."

"Did he mention anything else? Any enemies he might have had?"

Hollis shakes his head and says slowly, "They killed him."

"Who, Mr. Mulwray? Who killed him?"

"Whoever's trying to keep me from finding out about what happened to the dam."

"What are you talking about?"

"Detective, don't you think it's odd that I went out to ask him about the dam and then, a week later, he's dead? I think someone's trying to cover their tracks."

"Because of something you've uncovered?"

Hollis considers this. He hasn't found out much of anything; he's no closer to having an answer about why the dam failed than he was last week.

"No, but maybe my asking questions is making someone nervous. As I told you, there's a lot at stake."

"I have to tell you, that's not what it looks like to me, Mr. Mulwray."

"And what does it look like to you, Detective?"

"There's no sign of forced entry or foul play. We found fifty dollars in one of his drawers. This wasn't a robbery and, by the looks of this dump, the guy was a nobody. The only person who maybe wanted him dead was himself."

"You're saying it was a suicide?"

The detective breaks into a small grin.

"We already knew who he was, okay? A neighbor

found him and phoned it in first thing this morning. That gave me a chance to make a few calls. And I learned a thing or two about Mr. Fowler."

"Like what?"

From the other room there's the sound of a flashbulb.

"Like, after the thing at the dam he became chief of police of Santa Paula. Only he didn't do such a good job and they fired him a few years later for being a drunk and stealing from the department."

Hollis shakes his head.

"That doesn't mean anything."

"His career in the pictures wasn't going so hot, either. From what I can tell, he hasn't done anything for five years except get paid peanuts for standing around in the background."

The detective can tell that Hollis isn't convinced.

"He was a sad man, Mr. Mulwray. There's a lot of that going around. Dying of a gun to the face these days is practically a natural cause."

"Detective, if you knew all this, why did you have me come down here? Why did you want me to look at the body?"

"I wanted to know what you know. Wanted to see how you were connected. How you reacted when you saw him."

"And what did you learn?"

"That you're in over your head, Mr. Mulwray."

Hollis feels his face go red.

"Am I free to go, Detective?"

"No, Mr. Mulwray, there's one more thing. I want to know why you lied to me."

Hollis doesn't say anything. From the other room, there's the sound of more flashbulbs.

"I don't know what you're talking about."

The detective, with a blank face, reaches into his suit jacket. He pulls out the small notebook he had the other day. He flips through the pages, looking for something.

"You told me you had a family. A daughter." He squints to read his own writing. "Katherine."

"So?"

"I did a little digging. You don't have a daughter, Mr. Mulwray. Nor does your wife."

Hollis shuts his eyes, tight.

"Detective, it's ... complicated."

"Mrs. Mulwray does, however, have a bad reputation. Seems there are all kinds of rumors floating around town about her."

Another flashbulb. Hollis flinches.

"And what does that have to do with anything, Detective?"

"It's just I heard that Mrs. Mulwray *also* spent some time in Mexico. About seventeen years ago." He looks back to the notebook and begins flipping through it.

"That reminds me. How old did you say that daughter of yours was?"

"That's quite enough, Mr. Holabird. If you don't have any more questions, I'd like to leave."

"That's it, Mr. Mulwray." He puts the notebook back into his pocket. "For now."

In a daze, Hollis drives to a diner a few blocks from Fowler's house. He stumbles in and orders a cheese sandwich and a coffee. While sipping at his coffee, he glances at the meal of the man sitting next to him. Steak and eggs. The meat, juice, and gristle remind him of what was left of Elmer Fowler's head. When his cheese sandwich arrives, all Hollis can do is pick at it.

"More coffee, sir?"

He looks up and sees a young waitress in a gray uniform. Her name tag reads ESSIE.

"Excuse me, ma'am. Your name is Essie?"

"Yeah," she says in a midwestern accent, "short for Estelle. Now how about that coffee?"

He just shakes his head and the waitress moves on to the next customer.

Short for Estelle. Hollis realizes it's a nickname. He tries to think of more names Essie might be short for, but all he can come up with is Esther. Now he has two names, Esther and Estelle. But they still don't mean anything. Hollis can't think of anyone, from back then or even now, with either name. He quickly recalls the night the dam failed. Why would a person who was stopped say *Essie*? Then it hits him. *SCE*. Essie isn't a person, it's a business. Southern California Edison. The man was saying he worked for the power company.

Hollis throws down a couple of quarters and rushes outside. He gets in the Buick and speeds back to Los Angeles.

The Edison building is on Grand across from the Biltmore hotel. It's a tall skyscraper made of granite and terracotta, topped with the words EDISON in huge letters on all four sides. Inside each of the letters is neon tubing, which is kept on all night. You can see the red glow for miles. J. C. Wyatt has been in charge of the power company since the late '20s. Hollis runs into him at least once a month at county meetings or social events.

Hollis walks briskly through the huge lobby of thirty-foot ceilings and marble on every surface. At the twelfth floor, he rushes up to where Wyatt's secretary sits outside a pair of large double doors.

"Sonya, hello, I'm running terribly late. Have they started without me?"

"You had an appointment, Mr. Mulwray?"

Hollis just nods, points to his watch, and rushes past

her. Before she can stop him, he opens one of the doors and slips inside.

Wyatt's office is almost twice as big as Hollis's. The desk sits in front of a large window that overlooks the city. There's a round table and chairs, bookshelves stacked with leatherbound volumes, and a scale model of Los Angeles that takes up almost half the space. The model's incredibly detailed, with power lines, freeways, and even a miniature version of the Hollywood sign in the hills.

Wyatt's at the table with three older men who look to be bankers. They're each wearing exquisitely tailored suits, and all of them are twenty pounds too heavy.

"Didn't realize we had anything scheduled for today, Hollis." He motions to the men. "Can't this wait?"

"No, Josiah, I'm sorry. It can't."

Wyatt turns to his guests and says, apologetically, "Gentlemen, why don't you wait for me down in the lobby. We'll continue this over lunch."

Wyatt's visitors rise and shuffle out of the office. The combined smell of their aftershave hangs in the room after they're gone.

"Well, Hollis, you have my attention. Now what the hell is so important?"

"Why did you do it, Josiah?"

"Why did I do what?"

"The Van der Lip. Why?"

"Hollis, sit down. You're not making any sense."

Hollis takes the suggestion and pulls out one of the leather chairs from the round table.

"A man was stopped speeding away from the Van der Lip Dam the night that it failed. He said he worked for your company."

After a second, Wyatt answers, "So?"

"You don't think that's suspicious?"

"Perhaps," Wyatt says, "but it's hardly proof."

When Hollis doesn't say anything, Wyatt continues.

"Hollis, just what exactly are you trying to say?"

"You can't deny that the dam took away millions of dollars from your company. After the two power stations went online, all Edison had contracts for were a few small towns outside the city limits."

Wyatt holds up his hands.

"Now, Hollis, wait a minute. I wasn't in charge back then, and you know it."

"Yes, Josiah, but you must have heard something over the years. The man who was stopped couldn't have been working alone."

Wyatt shakes his head.

"Hollis, you're not making a bit of sense. The dam failed and people died. It's a tragedy, but we didn't cause it."

"Then who did?"

"Nobody, Hollis. These things just happen."

Looking down at his feet, Hollis sees blood on one of his shoes.

"We all looked for reasons," Wyatt continues. "Study after study was done. The papers reported every kind of crazy theory. Lunatics came out of the woodwork, remember? In the end, nobody could say for sure what happened."

"But the speeding car. This man."

"The one who was stopped that night? Maybe he did work for us. Or maybe he was just lying, Hollis, to get out of a ticket. People do it all the time. Either way, I can guarantee you that my company had nothing to do with your dam coming down."

"You're sure about that?"

"As sure as I can be about anything."

Not knowing what else to say, Hollis stands up.

Breathing a sigh of relief, Wyatt stands up, too. As he notices Hollis staring at the scale model of the city, he says, "Amazing, isn't it?"

Like an excited child eager to show off a toy, Wyatt hustles to one end of the display and flips a switch. The whole city lights up, including streetcars, apartment buildings and—glowing the brightest—the small red EDISON signs on the miniature version of the building they're standing in.

Hollis walks over to the table and examines the model more closely.

"Josiah?"

"Yes, Hollis?"

He points to a far edge, where a long row of power lines stretches over two square feet of flat brown that lie beyond a mountain range.

"The northeast valley," Hollis says. "Why are you extending lines all the way out there? There's nobody there. No houses, no buildings, nothing."

"Not yet there isn't."

"What do you mean?"

"Let's just say I got a tip."

"A tip?" Hollis says. "From whom?"

"Al Dill. You know him?"

Hollis remembers the editorial in the *Examiner* last week. "We Need Water Now."

"Alistair Dill?"

"That's him. He supplied me with a little, shall we say, *inside* information."

Hollis remembers the SOLD signs on acre after acre of dirt when he drove out to see Chester Grunsky.

Wyatt winks and says with a laugh, "Come on, walk me out."

Hollis turns and follows Wyatt out of the office in a daze.

As they're leaving, he says to his secretary, "Sonya, call Bernstein's and tell them to get a booth ready for me and the boys."

She nods and picks up the phone as they enter the elevator.

Descending to the lobby, Wyatt says, "I can get you in if you want."

"With what?"

"Dill and the boys. Most of the good parcels are gone, but I could make a few calls. If your father-in-law hasn't done that already."

Hollis doesn't say anything.

In the lobby, Wyatt's guests are laughing and puffing on cigars.

"Gentlemen." Wyatt wrings his hands. "Let's eat!"

That night, at dinner, all Evelyn can talk about is Katherine.

"You should go and visit her, Hollis."

"I will, darling, I told you." He stares down at his untouched prime rib. He still doesn't have an appetite. "Wednesday. Tomorrow's a busy day with the hearing, and then I have to drive out to a few reservoirs. But Wednesday I should be able to. The whole morning will be hers."

"Could you maybe take her shopping or something? She has absolutely nothing to wear."

"So, then what was in all of those trunks and luggage?"

Evelyn doesn't answer; she just pushes away her plate and reaches for a pack of Lucky Strikes.

As she lights a cigarette, Hollis considers telling her about earlier. The discussion with the detective. After all, Holabird might show up at the house asking uncomfortable questions about Katherine. What would they say? Where would they send her this time? But he doesn't, figuring Evelyn's already worried enough. No need to make things worse.

She quickly stubs out the cigarette and stands up.

"I'm not hungry. I'm going to go upstairs and lie down for a bit."

"I think that's a good idea."

As Evelyn leaves, Kahn enters the room. He looks worried.

"Everything okay, Mr. Mulwray?"

"Yes, Kahn. She's just a little tired."

The butler is leaving when Hollis calls after him.

"Kahn, could you get me a cocktail?"

"Of course, Mr. Mulwray. An old-fashioned?"

"No," Hollis says, getting up and heading to the patio. He wants to check on the pond. "Vodka daiquiri."

Hollis is late for the city council meeting because he stopped off to buy a pint of Four Roses for the man he met at the river last week. After the hearing, Hollis is going to drop by Hollenbeck Bridge and then check out a number of reservoirs. He'd called the regional directors the day before, but each insisted they'd only been following Hollis's written orders. Jack Tanner paid him a visit that morning, telling Hollis there'd been more calls about water being drained at various places around the county. As he left for city hall, Yelburton finally turned up. He claimed to not know about the reservoirs, Elwin, or much of anything. His delivery was so smooth, Hollis almost believed him.

After he hustles up the stone steps, a clerk directs him to a courtroom on the ground floor. Everyone's already seated and waiting for him. Hollis places his leather briefcase on the long table and takes a seat next to Sam Bagby, their backs to the council president and a huge portrait of FDR. Bagby, wearing a dark-brown double-breasted suit, looks smug and confident. He winks at Hollis after he sits down. Indeed, everyone's treating the construction of the dam like a foregone conclusion. Even the bond issue seems assured.

The deputy chairman stands and begins to make his opening remarks into a large microphone. His southern drawl echoes throughout the cavernous room. As he drones on about the assorted rules of order, and the morning's schedule of votes, a few of the council members sitting at the tables facing the stage continue reading comics and gossip columns.

Hollis looks out into the audience. Nobody there seems very engaged, either. Four rows back, on the left, a smartly dressed man reads the *Racing Form*. Others fan themselves with their hats, trying to stay cool. The only people paying any attention are a number of farmers who have gathered to hear their fate. For Bagby and the councilmen, the dam is just one move in a chess game. For the farmers, and people who will live in the shadow of the new dam, it's a matter of life and death.

Bagby's called first to speak. He limps to a huge map of the proposed Alto Vallejo Dam and Reservoir. He reiterates what he and his minions have been saying in the press for months: the city needs water.

When it's his turn to speak, Hollis grabs a sheet of notes from a file folder and walks to the plans for the dam. He points out the flaws he knows exist, the ones everyone else is willing to overlook. He tells the room it's the Van der Lip all over again, and he's not going to build it. Hollis can sense the tension. The farmers are angry. Bagby is angry. The council president wrings his hands. Hollis doesn't care; five hundred lives are enough.

As he steps down from the dais, there's a commotion toward the front of the room. The huge double doors open with a crash as two men—farmers—rush inside. One of them, wearing a weathered brown fedora and black suspenders, directs a dozen sheep to run toward the front of the chambers. The other man, deeply tanned and carrying a shepherd's crook with a twisted antler at the end, bustles down the aisle between the row of seats as the sheep charge ahead.

A bailiff in the corner, old and fat, gets out of his chair but makes no other move. There's pandemonium as the deputy chairman calls for order, men in the gallery shout or break into laughter, and the animals bray and scratch at the floor with their hooves. The man with the crook, restrained by two guards, begins to shout. It takes Hollis, his glasses off and somewhat in a daze, a few seconds to realize that the man is shouting at him.

"What are you doing with the water, Mr. Mulwray?"

A sergeant at arms restrains the man and tries to drag him out of the chambers, but he resists. Standing up, Hollis can see the man's leathery face turning red as the hands on him begin to pull him back. But still he shouts.

"Who's paying you, Mr. Mulwray?"

Both farmers are forcibly removed from the room, but the sheep remain. They run side to side along the rows, men raising their legs to let them by. Others continue to charge up and down the aisle, slipping on the slick floor. A few jump the low partition from the gallery to the tables and small stage, the sheep mingling among the drowsy city council members.

Due to the commotion, the deputy chairman—much to Bagby's chagrin—postpones the vote until later in the week. Grinning, Hollis grabs his briefcase and rushes for the exit. Bagby and a few others try to get his attention, but Hollis ignores them.

Outside, the sun is beating down. Hollis can feel heat

rising from the sidewalk. As he turns the corner onto Temple and sees his Buick parked at the end of the block, he also spots the farmer with the shepherd's crook. He's standing next to a weathered green truck. The truck's tailgate is down, and two men in work clothes are getting the last of a dozen or so sheep to walk up a ramp and into the back of the truck.

Next to the farmer is a man who looks vaguely familiar. He's tall and is wearing overalls and dusty boots. Hollis recognizes him as Chester Grunsky, the man he spoke to last week in the valley, one of the trio who quit their jobs at the Van der Lip Dam the day it came down. Grunsky's laughing and patting the other farmer on the back.

Incensed, Hollis tries to cross the street in order to confront Grunsky, but a truck and then two taxis block his path. By the time the traffic clears, the green truck is pulling away from the curb. The sheep in the back bleat as the sun bears down on them without mercy.

Hollis sighs and steps back onto the sidewalk. As he approaches his car, he sees that something's tucked underneath the windshield wipers. Stepping up to the Buick, he grabs the piece of paper. POINT FERMIN. THE BEACH. TONIGHT. COME ALONE. The paper is cream-colored and the loping handwriting—which Hollis doesn't recognize—is in blue ink. Hollis folds the paper into quarters, puts it into his jacket, and gets into the car.

Hollis once again guides the Buick down the long sloping dirt path that runs underneath Hollenbeck Bridge. He parks, wipes his forehead with a handkerchief, and gets out of the car. The pool of water from last week is mostly gone. Today, the only trace is some dark, moist sand around the storm drain.

"Hello?"

Hollis approaches where he saw the man last week. Bending at the waist, he peers into the lean-to. He sees a few empty bottles of liquor, a wooden brush, two tin cups, and a cracked plate.

"Anybody home?"

When there's no answer, Hollis takes the pint of whiskey from his hip pocket and places it on the dresser. Walking back to the Buick, he sees a dark-skinned boy riding bareback on a light-gray horse. He's coming from the other side of the river. The horse is old and moves slowly over the hot, dry riverbed. Hollis yells out and approaches the boy.

"Excuse me, do you speak English?"

The boy, wearing a large straw hat and a billowy cotton shirt, nods his head, yes.

"The man who lives under the bridge, have you seen him lately?"

"Not since two days ago. He left when the water came."

"More water? How much was it?"

The boy shrugs.

"Flooded his camp. Almost flooded ours, too."

"When was this?"

The boy looks up to the sky as he tries to remember.

"Friday, then again on Sunday."

Hollis points at the ground.

"Right at this spot?"

The boy shakes his head.

"It's a different spot every night."

"Was it a lot?"

"Enough to drive the man away."

"And how about for your family?"

The boy shrugs again.

"We have nowhere else to go."

The boy tugs on the horse's rein—which is merely a loop of rope around the animal's neck—and heads back in the direction of his camp. Hollis walks to the Buick and pulls from the back seat the big book of blueprints he brought from his office. With a red pencil he makes a few notes. After he places the book back in the car, Hollis once again wipes the sweat from his forehead. After he puts the handkerchief back into his pocket, he looks at his watch: 1:24. If he hurries, he should just about catch Noah Cross as he's finishing lunch.

Hollis spots the Pig 'n Whistle from a block away; the bright-red sign and huge pink plaster pig playing a flute are hard to miss. Hollis parks and approaches as diners enter and leave. Peering in from the sidewalk, he can see the black-and-white tiled floor, candy counter, and customers seated at barstools eating sundaes. Tables and booths are toward the rear. Noah's favorite spot is in the far corner. He likes to sit with his back to the wall, linger over his shirred eggs and fried onions, and survey the room. The ordinary citizen may have forgotten who he is, but friends and associates often stop by to pay their respects. Just like the old days.

After a few minutes of waiting, Cross emerges with two other men about his age. He's wearing a dark three-piece suit, black tie embroidered with fish heads, and a tan hat. In his left hand he clutches an unlit cigar. In his right, he carries a cane with a gold handle.

"I'll see you gentlemen next week."

After they all nod to each other, the two men head west down Hollywood Boulevard while Cross begins to walk east, toward where his chauffeur's parked in an alley.

"Noah," Hollis says, stepping forward, "I'd like to speak with you."

Cross turns and smiles, his yellow teeth bared like an animal.

"Why, Mr. Mulwray, splendid to see you. How are you?"

He offers his hand, but Hollis doesn't take it.

"Let's spare the pleasantries."

"As you wish. What can I do for you?"

As a family emerges from the Pig 'n Whistle and begins to pass them, Hollis leans toward Cross and says in a whisper, "I know what you're doing. You and everyone else from that club of yours."

The hand with the cane rises and cups Cross's ear.

"What's that?"

"Albacore!" Hollis shouts. "I know what you're up to, you and your damn friends."

Cross is embarrassed by the outburst.

"Hollis, please. Shall we go back inside and discuss it?"

"No, Noah."

The old man gestures to the idling car.

"Then perhaps a drive?"

"I'm not going anywhere with you."

Resigned to having the conversation in public, Cross takes a deep breath.

"Me and my damn friends, as you see fit to describe them, made this city. With your help, as I remember."

"Anything I did, I did for the people and not to line my own pockets."

Cross steps back and leans on his cane, examining his son-in-law.

"Your pockets seem very stylish, Mr. Mulwray. I do believe that's a hand-tailored suit. What did it cost you?"

"Go to hell, Noah."

"Maybe one day, Hollis, but not today."

Hollis begins to walk away when Cross calls after him.

"How's my daughter?"

He stops and turns back to the old man. He's smiling and once again leaning on his cane.

"Evelyn is fine, thank you for asking."

"I still care for her very deeply. I don't want to see her getting hurt."

"That's rich, coming from you, Noah."

Cross puts the cigar in his mouth and says, "Whatever happened all those years ago, she's still my daughter. They both are."

Hollis opens his mouth to reply, but nothing comes out.

Pleased with Hollis's stunned silence, Cross shuffles toward the car. A dark-skinned driver jumps out and opens the passenger door. The driver closes the door and then resumes his place behind the wheel. The car disappears down the alley as more customers enter and exit the Pig 'n Whistle.

Driving out to the Oak Pass Reservoir, Hollis notices he's being followed. A large black sedan appears behind him as he pulls away from Hollywood Boulevard. Looking in the rearview mirror, Hollis sees that it's an older man, balding and with glasses. Even after he turns onto the winding mountain road that leads to the reservoir, the car is still there. It's only when Hollis turns onto a dirt trail hemmed in by oak and eucalyptus trees that the car continues going straight. He waits for a few minutes, to see if it passes by in the other direction, but it never does.

Convinced the car's not coming back, he continues down the dirt road until it dead-ends at a chain-link fence. Hollis stops the car and gets out. A padlock and length of chain are on the ground, and the metal gate in the fence swings back and forth in the wind. A faded wooden sign hangs crooked above the entrance. OAK PASS RESERVOIR. KEEP OUT. NO TRESPASSING.

Hollis looks around for the guards Russ hired. That man, Mulvihill, or his associates. But there's no one. He passes through the gate and examines the dozen flood channels. More than half of them appear to have been used recently, probably the night before.

He goes back to the Buick and once again pulls out

the book of blueprints. With the red pencil he writes, *Tues. Oak Pass Res. — 7 channels used*. He puts the book back in the car and drives out to the Stone Canyon Reservoir. There's traffic, and he has to go all the way across town, so it takes him more than an hour. Once there, Hollis finds the same thing. No one's around, the gate is open, and the levels are way lower than they should be. Examining the channels, he sees footprints. Someone has been here recently. After making more notes in the book of blueprints, he places it back into the car.

Leaning against the Buick, Hollis pulls out of his suit jacket the note he found on his windshield that morning. POINT FERMIN. THE BEACH. TONIGHT. COME ALONE. He doesn't know whether it's a trap or will finally provide some answers. Time is running out, and if he's ever going to know what happened at Van der Lip, it needs to happen soon. He glances at his watch: 5:05. Hollis figures he can grab a sandwich on the way out of Los Angeles, call Evelyn from a pay phone, and be at San Pedro by dusk.

The sun's just beginning to set as he enters Point Fermin Park. Driving down Paseo Del Mar Road, Hollis passes families finishing picnics and children flying kites in the cool ocean breeze. The road dead-ends just past a small café. As he parks the car, he hears music coming from the café. The voice of Bing Crosby floats into the night, mixing with the sound of the waves hitting the rocks below. He gets out of the Buick and approaches the steep bluffs that lead to the water.

There's a chain-link fence at the end of the street, but it's wide open. Hollis looks to the right and sees the old lighthouse. It looks like any Victorian home you might see in San Francisco. White picket fence, gabled roof, porch railings. The lighthouse on the third story just looks like a big window.

As Hollis begins to step carefully down the hill to get to the shore, there's a gust of wind and he has to hold on to his hat to keep it from flying off. Halfway down the hill is a large metal outfall pipe. Pipes like these run up and down the coast, connected to drains and sewers. After another few cautious steps—dirt and rocks give way with every step—he reaches the bottom. Unlike sandy beaches to the north or south, the shore here is made up of flat black rocks and shallow tidal pools.

Standing near the water, he's not quite sure what to do next. The note didn't specify an exact time, or what to do once he got here. So he just waits and feels self-conscious in his double-breasted suit and bow tie. At the sound of falling rocks, he quickly looks back to the bluffs. He's still paranoid after being followed over the weekend, and then earlier today, but he doesn't see anything. He turns back to the ocean.

Hollis has been here before. As a child, a long time ago. There'd been a funeral for an uncle in Long Beach, and he and his parents had taken the train down and stayed with relatives for a week. Before heading back to Monterey his father, knowing Hollis's fondness for tidal pools, insisted they come out here. The lighthouse was relatively new back then, had been in operation for only a few years. Hollis recalls the house as being blindingly white. San Pedro was just a quiet fishing village at the time. On the streetcar ride over, they saw more boats than houses. But they'd mistimed their visit. The tide wasn't yet out, so there wasn't much to see. All Hollis remembers is the white lighthouse, the black rocks, and the feel of his father's strong grip as they descended the bluffs, his dad repeating, "Trust me, Son," all the way down.

On one of the rocks, Hollis sees a starfish. He kneels down to pick it up. He's long been fascinated by them. They have no brain, no blood, and there's an eye at the end of each arm. He used to draw pictures of them as a child and place them all around his room.

When he hears water begin to trickle from the outfall pipe, he sets the starfish down and turns back to the steep hill. The trickle soon turns into gushing as water shoots out of the pipe, turning the sand of the hill into mud as the water travels to the shore. Hollis watches this dispassionately before turning back to the shore to see the sun slowly set.

After an hour of nothing, Hollis hears something. An engine. He looks up, thinking it's a seaplane. They fly almost nonstop from Los Angeles to Catalina filled with fishermen, gamblers, vacationers. But the night sky is clear; all Hollis sees is the moon. He looks back up toward the bluffs, but there's nothing there, either.

Finally, out in the waves, he sees a light. A boat is slowly approaching. It's too far out for Hollis to see who's aboard, but he recognizes it as a fishing boat. It stops fifty yards from the shore. A minute later, he watches as a dinghy is lowered into the water. The dinghy nears the rocks, heading right for him. Squinting, Hollis sees a man with a hat and a long overcoat standing up in the small boat. A second man, short and stocky and wearing work clothes, sits and operates the small engine. The dinghy pulls into the cove.

"Mr. Mulwray!"

As Hollis ventures further onto the rocks, he recognizes the man in the overcoat as Wallace Holabird.

"Detective," Hollis says incredulously, "what are you doing here?"

"I've come for you, Mr. Mulwray."

"What? Why?"

"Get in the boat, please."

As Hollis weighs his options, the detective pulls back

his overcoat and suit jacket to reveal a pistol in a brown leather shoulder holster. Hollis raises his hands slightly and approaches the dinghy.

The detective holds out an arm and Hollis leaps from the rocks onto the small boat, grabbing the man to steady himself. The dinghy sways but doesn't overturn.

The detective calls out to the man at the engine, "Take us in, Curly."

The small boat is steered away from the rocks and back into the waves. It takes only a minute to pull up alongside the fishing boat. The detective gets off first, and then turns to help Hollis. Hollis steps aboard as the other man ties up the dinghy.

The smell of bait and fish hovers over the deck. The detective keeps his eyes on Hollis as the man in work clothes hops aboard and scampers to the helm. The engines start up and the boat slowly turns away from the coast.

"So, Detective, where are we going?"

"Albacore Club. A few folks would like to have a word with you."

"Is this official police business, or are you freelancing?"

The detective doesn't say anything, he just grins.

"How much are they paying you, Detective?"

Still grinning, he says, "Remember when I told you I moved to Los Angeles for my health?"

"Yes."

"Well, going against these men would be bad for my health."

As the boat rises and falls on the choppy waters, Hollis glances up to the man at the helm. He doesn't look back, or even acknowledge the conversation happening around him.

"What's going to happen," Hollis continues, "when I call headquarters tomorrow and tell your sergeant about all of this?"

"Go right ahead, Mr. Mulwray. In fact, I bet you'll see the chief of police there tonight. He's a good friend of the local sheriff." The detective pulls out a pack of cigarettes and has to turn against the wind in order to light one. Exhaling, he says, "Just settle in, Mr. Mulwray, and enjoy the ride."

Hollis walks to the rear of the boat and turns up his collar to the freezing mist. Looking back at San Pedro, he can see the lights of the StarKist cannery. The city, just beyond, is a dull glow. It's still not a very big town.

An hour later, the detective says, "Mr. Mulwray, we're here."

Hollis turns and can tell they're coming around Casino Point. The huge round building is brightly lit, its reflection dancing on the water. As they pass by, Hollis can hear the shouting of gamblers and revelers. The fishing boat pulls into the harbor. Just beyond the dozen or so boats, he sees the Albacore Club. The blue-and-white clapboard building looks purple in the moonlight. Even though Cross owns an elaborate home on the island called Rancho del Cruce, this is where he spends most of his time.

"Mr. Mulwray, if you'll kindly follow me."

The detective hops off the boat and walks up the ramp toward the club. Hollis follows close behind. On the glass panes of the double doors, it says MEMBERS ONLY. The detective continues to lead the way, walking through the main dining room toward a back room, which Hollis knows from experience is where Cross spends most of his time.

The detective opens the door and then stands aside for Hollis to enter. After Hollis steps into the room, the door is closed behind him. There are a few wingback chairs and a sofa arranged around a lit fireplace, but everyone's seated at a large round table positioned in front of a window that runs the length of the room. Normally, the window gives a striking view of the bay—on a clear day you can see all the way to San Diego—but since it's dark outside, it just reflects the backs of the men.

Other than Noah Cross, the only person Hollis recognizes is Sam Bagby. Sitting on the left with his back to the fireplace, Bagby's still wearing the brown suit from this morning. He somehow looks even more smug and confident than he did at city hall. The tabletop is filled with empty and half-filled cocktails. A number of the men are smoking cigars.

"Ah, Hollis," Noah calls out, "good to see you again."

Hollis approaches the table warily.

"You're now adding kidnapping to your list of moral transgressions, are you, Noah?"

"Well, after your performance at the city council meeting this morning, we all felt that a little persuasion was called for." He motions to the men seated around the table. "Let me introduce the boys."

Noah rises—having to lean on his gold-topped cane to do so—and proceeds to call out each man's name, like a teacher taking attendance.

"We have Charles Knox, Jo Stoyte, Alistair Dill, Abe Speer, and Eli Crabb. Sam Bagby, I believe, you know already."

Even though they're all different ages—some are well into their seventies, while a few aren't even forty—they all look the same: rich, soft, privileged.

"Dill," Hollis repeats, turning to a plump man with a baby face, "I heard you gave a tip to J. C. Wyatt about some land."

"I gave him more than a tip."

Dill laughs and takes another puff off his cigar.

Cross sits down and says, "You see, Hollis, we're just about to get the question of the water supply all wrapped up. The bond issue and the dam will take care of that. But we also need electricity. That's why Wyatt was brought on board."

"And he no doubt bought a bit of land for himself."

"I'm sure he did. We all have." Cross points to various men around the table. "Al over there bought twelve thousand acres. Eli bought twenty-five. Abe and Jo and Charles got some as well, but not as much."

"Not this time," says Stoyte.

"Yes, sorry about that, Jo. But tell Hollis about last year."

The man, who looks to be in his sixties, beams with pride as he speaks. "I got a tip they were going to pipe water into the San Felipe Valley. Enough to irrigate the whole valley. Ended up buying thirty thousand acres for twelve bucks an acre. Kept my name out of it, of course. Didn't want that to be a distraction."

Cross asks through a smile, "And how much is that land worth now, Jo?"

Stoyte answers, "Millions."

"You see, Hollis," continues Cross, "that's just business. It's the way Los Angeles has functioned since the pueblo days, and I'm sure that's how it will function long after you and I are both gone. It's just the way things work."

"Even if you have to break the law to do it?"

Everyone in the room except Hollis bursts into laughter.

"We don't break the law, Hollis, we make the law. Hell"—Cross looks around the room—"we *are* the law."

All the smoke in the room is making Hollis nauseous. He also feels clammy after coming in from the cold of the fishing boat to the overheated room. But he's determined to not show any weakness. He stands up as straight as he can and says firmly, "I don't care what kind of shenanigans you and your cronies here have got going on as a sideline, I'm not going to build that dam."

Each of the men slowly turns his head toward Cross.

"Hollis, most people don't know the difference between shale and schist. However, the men in this room—I'm delighted to say—own two newspapers, a film studio, and a radio station. If *we* say it's safe, then it's safe."

"And what if it crumbles again, just like last time? Are you going to let another five hundred people die?"

"Hollis," Cross sighs, "you need to forget about the Van der Lip. What's past is past. You can't bring those people back."

Each of the men slowly turns his head back to Hollis.

"Maybe not, Noah. But I don't have to pile on more bodies." Before Cross or anyone can respond, he adds, "Will there be anything else, or may I leave?"

"You may go."

Hollis turns and leaves the room.

The detective doesn't say anything on the way back to

Point Fermin, and the man steering the boat doesn't say anything, either. When Hollis jumps off the dinghy more than an hour later, the detective calls out, "Good night, Mr. Mulwray," but his voice is nearly drowned out by the surf.

After he climbs up the bluffs, Hollis finds the street completely empty. The café's closed and there's not another car on the block. Approaching the Buick, he sees—yet again—something tucked under the windshield. It's a flyer printed on cheap paper. SAVE OUR CITY! LOS ANGELES IS DYING OF THIRST! PROTECT YOUR PROPERTY!

Hollis crumples it into a ball and lets it fall to the black pavement.

"WHAT ABOUT THIS one, Papa?"

Katherine points to a teal dress displayed in a glass case on a rosewood stand. They're shopping at Bullock's, the huge department store at Wilshire and Vermont. It feels to Hollis like they've been here for hours.

"It's lovely, sweetheart, but I liked the last three dresses you showed me, too."

She gives a small frown and continues down the aisle. Her head darts back and forth as she takes in the various styles and colors.

Hollis has only been to Bullock's once or twice, but

Evelyn comes here often. She spends most of her time shopping for designer dresses in the Louis XVI Room. Afterward, she and her friends have lunch in the formal tearoom on the fifth floor.

"Oh, Papa, how about this one?"

Katherine points to a dress that looks identical to the white one she's wearing, except it has a pattern of yellow roses.

"It's lovely. Would you like to try it on?"

She nods eagerly. Hollis flags down a salesgirl, who leads Katherine to a fitting room.

While he's waiting, Hollis wanders around the store. After a few steps he finds himself in the lingerie section. Glancing to see if anyone's watching, he begins to peruse the aisles of satin and lace. He considers buying something for Sadie. He's called her house three times in the past couple of days, but Frank answered each time. But maybe he could drop something off at the Cocoanut Grove, along with a note. He finally decides against it, not wanting to have to lie to Katherine about what it is.

When she finds him ten minutes later, amid a display of shoes, the dress is folded over her right arm.

"I love it, Papa. Will you buy it for me?"

"Don't I get to see it on you?"

"Later. After lunch."

He pays for the dress, and they ride the elevator to the

lobby. It's old-fashioned, with a uniformed attendant and an iron grating that's pulled open at every stop.

"First floor. Perfume Hall, menswear, and sportswear. Please watch your step."

They exit the elevator and walk through the marbled foyer, on their way to the rear entrance of the store, which opens onto the parking lot.

Standing in the porte cochere while they wait for the boy to return with the Buick, Katherine leans against Hollis and says, "Can we do something else now, Papa?"

"I thought you said you were going to make me lunch."

"Later, I want to do something else first."

"And what's that?"

The attendant pulls up with the Buick, and Hollis hands him a tip. Getting into the car, Katherine says, "You'll see."

Forty minutes later they're standing in line to rent a rowboat at Echo Park. Katherine is beaming; Hollis looks slightly embarrassed. It's a gorgeous day—not too hot and clear blue skies—so the lake is crowded with boats. The man running the concession sweats as he runs back and forth, collecting fees and helping customers into newly vacated boats. Hollis and Katherine are third in line.

"How did you even hear of this, Katherine? You've only been in town for a week."

"I heard some people at the apartment building talking about it. They said it was a fun thing to do."

A young couple at the front of the line are pointed to a boat. They skip down the pier holding hands. Hollis and Katherine take a few steps forward.

"Are there many people there your age?"

"A few. I think they're actors."

"Why do you say that?"

"I heard them in the courtyard reciting lines back and forth. I think it was for a movie, or I suppose it could have been a play."

A mother and her young son are pointed to a newly freed boat. Hollis and Katherine are next.

"Do you think you'd like to try acting?" he says.

"I don't know. It sure looks easy. And I think it'd be fun to be someone else for a while."

Three teenagers pull up to the pier and hop out of a boat with a black number 5 painted on the stern. All the boats are painted green on the inside and white on the outside. As the teenagers pass by, each of them giggling, Hollis hands over a few coins. He and Katherine walk down the short pier. Hollis gets in first and takes Katherine's hand as she steps into the small boat. He sits down, grabs hold of the oars, and guides them onto the lake.

Once they're clear of the pier, he says, "You know, this lake started as a reservoir."

"Really, Papa? Was it one of yours?"

"No," he says as he continues to row, "that was another company. And it was well before my time. Was just a big ditch. Later they turned it into this lake."

Hollis has to keep glancing behind him to make sure he doesn't run into other boaters. The green water is bounded on all sides by palm trees and, just beyond, there are cement sidewalks, picnic benches, and swathes of grass.

"They used to make movies around here, too."

"What kind?"

"Silent ones, comedies. Keystone Cops and pies in the face, that kind of thing."

Katherine makes a face.

"If I did try acting, that's not the kind of movie *I'd* like to be in."

As they float underneath a wooden bridge painted the same color green as the boats, Hollis thinks of Elmer Fowler standing in the sun out in Chatsworth on the set of a Shirley Temple film. He says, "Well, sweetheart, I don't know if you get to exactly *choose* what kind of movies you're in. At least not at the beginning."

Katherine disregards this and says, "Can we go to the movies sometime, Papa?"

"Of course, sweetheart. We have plenty of time."

Hearing this, she sits back and turns her face to the sun. For the first time since she came to Los Angeles, she seems truly comfortable. Her happiness is infectious. Hollis breaks into a smile as he rows past two men in dapper suits, one of whom is photographing the other.

After three laps around the lake, Katherine is satisfied and Hollis is exhausted. They return the rowboat and drive back to El Macando. Hollis relaxes on the patio reading a newspaper as Katherine makes lunch. She sings while she cooks, and he discovers she has a wonderful voice. Maybe she could make it as an actress. He doesn't have any contacts, but Evelyn knows people. Maybe she could make some calls, get Katherine a few auditions.

"Are you ready?"

He puts down the newspaper he'd brought from the car and calls back, "Yes, sweetheart."

Katherine carries out two plates laden with food. Chicken in some sort of dark sauce served with rice and vegetables. It smells delicious. When Katherine places the meal on the metal table, Hollis can see how proud she is.

"Sweetheart, this looks amazing."

Katherine sits down and they both dig in. After a few forkfuls, Hollis—still chewing—asks, "How did you learn how to make this?"

"The cooks at school taught me."

"But when?"

"Oh, weekends. You know, after class. Things like that."

He takes another bite.

"And that's how you learned to speak Spanish?"

She nods. After swallowing, she adds, "And we go into town. You know, to markets and places. I once saw an entire movie in Spanish. I didn't understand everything, but I got most of it."

Hollis smiles, impressed.

"You should learn some, Papa."

He cuts another piece of chicken, dipping it into the sauce.

"I've tried before, it's hard."

"No, you can do it. I'll help you."

"How?"

"For the rest of the afternoon, we'll speak only Spanish."

He laughs.

"Then I'm afraid I won't be able to say very much."

Katherine stabs a few vegetables and holds up her fork.

"Me gusta este plato. ¿Cómo lo hiciste?"

Her accent is flawless. If Hollis heard her speaking at the house, he'd assume it was one of the servants.

"Now you try it, Papa."

When Hollis repeats the phrase as well as he can, Katherine breaks into laughter.

"Okay," she says, "here's something easier. If you like something, just say *me gusta*."

"*Me gusta*," Hollis repeats.

"That was wonderful, Papa." Katherine claps. "Try again."

He says it again.

"That was perfect. You just need to practice, that's all."

When they're done eating, Hollis begins to gather the plates. Katherine stops him.

"Papa, just leave those."

"Are you sure?"

"Yes. You just sit and read your paper. I'll make some coffee and then show you my new dress."

"Okay, sweetheart, but after that I have to leave."

She smiles and quickly enters the apartment. He returns to the newspaper. He's halfway through a story about Amelia Earhart when he hears Katherine from the apartment.

"*Tápate los ojos.*"

"What's that, dear?"

"Cover your eyes."

He puts down the paper again, flattens each hand, and places them in front of his face. He hears Katherine's heels on the red brick of the patio.

"*Puedes mirar ahora.*"

He drops his hands. The dress fits perfectly.

As she twirls and sways, she says, *"Te gusta?"*

Hollis rises out of the chair.

"Me gusta."

As he leans in for an embrace, he hears a noise, something breaking. Hollis looks around. He doesn't see anything but trees and the terra-cotta roof of the building next door. He turns back to Katherine. Her smile is bigger than ever.

That night, they don't say much during dinner. Hollis briefly mentions the morning and afternoon with Katherine, and Evelyn tells him about her lunch with friends at the Jonathan Club. After dinner they take their cocktails into the library, the way they do most evenings.

At a few minutes past ten o'clock, the butler enters the room.

"Mr. Mulwray, there's a telephone call for you. Someone from the *Evening Post-Record*."

"In my day," Evelyn says, "they used to send the paperboy to collect on subscriptions."

As Hollis reaches for the receiver, she stubs out her cigarette and stands up. On her way out of the room, she says quietly, "I'll see you upstairs."

Hollis is still nodding at her when he hears the voice on the phone say, "Mr. Mulwray?"

"Yes."

"Hollis Mulwray?"

It's a man. In the background Hollis can hear various discussions and what sounds like typing.

"Yes, how can I help you?"

"My name is Leighton Early, and I'm a reporter for the *Los Angeles Evening Post-Record*. I'd like to get a comment from you on a story we're going to run in tomorrow's paper."

Because of the drought, heat wave, and the upcoming bond issue about the dam, Hollis has actually seen his name in the papers quite a lot lately. However, it's usually in one-sided hit pieces or editorials, like Alistair Dill's from last week. Reporters rarely call to get his side of the story.

"Okay, Mr. Early, what's the article going to say?"

The reporter shuffles papers as he prepares to read.

"The headline is 'Department of Water and Power Blows Fuse over Chief's Use of Funds for El Macando Love Nest.'"

"Good God," Hollis gasps.

"Is that your official comment, Mr. Mulwray?"

"Mr. Early, I can assure you, it's not what you think. You have to believe me."

"Well, Mr. Mulwray, I'd like to believe you, except that

earlier tonight we were sent a number of photos of you and a young woman. Some were taken in a boat in Echo Park, and others were taken at an apartment building in Los Feliz."

"How did you—who sent you these photos?"

"I'm afraid I'm not at liberty to say. However, I will tell you that, after we received the tip, I sent a man down to the apartment to see who lived there. Unfortunately, we don't have the name of the girl, seeing as how the apartment was leased in *your* name. But our man did uncover something rather interesting."

"And what's that?"

"The apartment's being paid for with department funds. The manager showed us a check, signed by you, drawn from a corporate account. Care to comment?"

Hollis tries to remember the story he told the building manager.

"She's an intern, from back east. A specialist. An engineer working on a new project."

"An engineer?" The reporter's voice is drenched in skepticism. "She looks a little young for that."

"Intern, I said. Intern."

"Okay then, you're having an affair with an intern. Congratulations."

Hollis takes off his glasses and rubs his eyes.

"Mr. Early, I'm telling you. This is *not* what it looks like."

There's silence for a second before the reporter replies.

"Well then, Mr. Mulwray, you tell me what's happening. Because I see you in the arms of a cheap-looking blonde on the patio of a second-rate apartment building. You were also seen together in a rowboat in Echo Park. We have photos. There's no use trying to deny it."

"It's not," he splutters, "we're not. We weren't—"

"I'll tell you what," the reporter interrupts. "If you give me her name, I'll talk to her. Get her side of the story. Maybe I can persuade my editor to put off the story for another day. Will you do that, let me talk to the girl?"

"No, I'm sorry, I can't—"

"Then this is the story we're going to run tomorrow in the morning edition. Now, for the final time, what can I print as your response, Mr. Mulwray?"

"No comment," Hollis finally answers.

After the reporter hangs up, Hollis just sits there, eyes closed tight and listening to the dial tone. He finally places the receiver back into the cradle.

Sighing heavily, he rises from the chair and walks upstairs. Passing by the dining room, he hears the servants in the kitchen cleaning up and speaking Spanish. Before entering the master bedroom, he looks across the hall to the guest room where Katherine had stayed.

"Darling?"

In bed with a copy of *Redbook*, Evelyn looks up.

"Yes?"

"That call from the *Post-Record*, it was a reporter. They're going to run a story tomorrow about me having an affair."

Her eyes turn to ice. Her entire face is frozen, like a mask.

"It's not what you think. They have photos, from earlier today, apparently. Of me and Katherine. At Echo Park and at the apartment building. They think she's my mistress."

Hollis walks toward the bed and sits down.

"Who was the reporter?" Evelyn says, putting the magazine down. "Do you know him?"

He shakes his head.

"Leighton Early. The name's familiar, though I've never met him in person."

"And you think it's real?"

"That what is real?"

"The phone call, the photos."

"What are you getting at?"

"Maybe someone's trying to trick you. To trick us."

"To do what?"

"To get to Katherine."

"Why? They already know about the apartment. Whether or not they have pictures, they know where she lives and that I was there with her."

"But the article still may just be a threat, or a hoax or something." She looks nervously toward the bedroom window that overlooks the backyard. "Maybe we're being watched right now."

Hollis thinks of the car that followed him yesterday to the reservoir.

"Maybe you're right. Maybe it's Bagby, or Noah, just trying to rattle us."

Evelyn turns quickly from the window to her husband.

"My . . . father? You think he might be involved?"

Hollis shrugs and pulls at his bow tie.

"I don't know, it's possible."

He considers mentioning last night, or the encounter at the Pig 'n Whistle, but he doesn't. It would only make her worry more.

"So, then what do we do?"

"We do nothing. We go to sleep." He places his hands on hers. "And in the morning, we see what's in the paper."

When she continues to look worried, he leans forward and kisses her forehead.

"Just watch," Hollis says. "I bet it doesn't lead to anything at all."

10

I N THE MORNING, Kahn's waiting for them downstairs. Staring at the hardwood floors, hands behind his back, he looks like a statue.

"The papers," he says slowly. "I put them in the living room."

"Thank you, Kahn," Evelyn says as Hollis brushes past them both on his way to the front of the house.

Three newspapers are on the coffee table. Hollis quickly pulls out the *Post-Record* and sits down on the couch. When he sees the front page, he nearly passes out. Underneath the banner headline is a heart-shaped photo of Hollis and Katherine on the patio of her apartment. His eyes move back and forth as he quickly scans the article.

"Nonsense," he says, "it's absolute nonsense."

Evelyn sits down beside him and asks, "What does it say?"

"Just what the reporter told me last night. They think Katherine's my mistress. And the manager showed them my check from the department. He hadn't deposited it. What a disgrace."

While Evelyn leans in to read the story, Hollis points to the headline of a related article to the left of the photograph: "J. J. Gittes Hired by Suspicious Spouse."

"That must be who Bagby or whoever hired."

"But why would anyone be following you around?"

"They're trying to get dirt on me. To force me to build that dam." Hollis sighs heavily. "What a fool I've been. To perhaps save hundreds of lives, I've ruined ours."

Evelyn turns from the story to her husband.

"Oh, Hollis, what should we do?"

He puts down the paper.

"You should go see your lawyer. Right now."

"But why?"

Hollis motions to the article about J. J. Gittes.

"This says you hired a private detective. That means Bagby or somebody hired someone to *pretend* to be you."

"Yes, so?"

"Maybe your lawyer can create a case out of that. In terms of this Gittes fellow, I mean."

"I'm sorry, Hollis," she says, exasperated, "I'm still not following."

"The private detective took some woman's word that she was you. Just by showing up at his office, you can prove you *didn't* hire him. If we threaten him, serving some sort of papers and implying that this Gittes might lose his license, maybe the detective will give us some information."

Evelyn reaches for a pack of Lucky Strikes.

"Hollis, I just don't know."

"I realize it's a long shot, dear, but it's the only thing we can do."

She lights the cigarette and inhales deeply.

"There's one more thing," he adds. "We need to move Katherine again."

"But, Hollis, why? She's not even mentioned."

Evelyn's right. The story refers to her only as Hollis's "mystery girl."

"Yes, but Noah will surely see the paper. He'll recognize her and, when he does, he'll pay her a visit."

At the mention of her father, Evelyn begins to shake. Hollis reaches out and places a hand on her shoulder.

"Sweetheart, don't worry. He's all the way out on Catalina. Even if he wanted to, he couldn't get out there before noon."

"But where will we take her?"

While he's thinking, Evelyn finishes the cigarette and lights another.

"Violet's."

"What?"

"Your friend with the plants, out in Santa Monica. Is she still up north?"

"Yes, she'll be in San Francisco for at least another two weeks."

"And it's a big place, right? You could stay there too if you had to?"

"Why yes, Hollis. It's a three-bedroom, I believe."

"Perfect." He reaches for a pad of paper and a pencil sitting next to the ashtray and hands them to his wife. "Write down the address. While you and your lawyer are paying a visit to that idiot of a detective, I'll go to the apartment and pick up Katherine."

She scribbles down the address, rips off the sheet from the pad, and hands it to him. *1412 Adelaide Drive.*

"It's above Santa Monica Canyon."

He folds the paper in half and slips it into his hip pocket.

"Okay, I'll go after I make a few calls."

"Are you sure that's safe? Shouldn't you go right now?"

"Evelyn, everyone I work with is going to read that story. I need to phone the office, reassure the board that everything's okay. Reporters are probably all over the lobby."

She reaches for yet another cigarette, but he stops her.

"Evelyn, it's going to be okay, I promise."

He leans in for a kiss. All he tastes is tobacco.

As Hollis walks up the winding cement path to Katherine's apartment building, the manager steps out from the mailboxes. He's grinning and holding a newspaper. Hollis can see himself on the front page.

"You old dog. I knew she was no intern."

"It's not what it appears, I assure you."

"Well, you're too late anyway. She's met somebody else."

As Hollis advances, the manager moves to block the path. Hollis shoves him aside.

Standing in front of Katherine's door, he hears voices. Hollis raps quickly with his knuckles.

"Katherine?"

The voices instantly stop. He knocks again.

"Katherine, open up."

She finally answers the door holding what looks to be a movie script. A good-looking young man, not more than twenty, sits on the couch. He's also holding a script.

"Papa? What are you doing here?"

"Get your things, Katherine, we're going."

The young man on the couch rises.

"Aw, come on, mister. She was just helping me rehearse."

Hollis ignores him and says to Katherine, "Pack a suitcase, we have to leave. Right now."

Bursting into tears, she flees to the bedroom to do what he says. Hollis enters the apartment and turns to the boy.

"It's time for you to go."

The young man, clutching his script, sulks out of the room.

Katherine appears a minute later with only one piece of her matching luggage.

"That's fine," Hollis says. "I'll send Kahn for the rest later."

Katherine pouts on the drive to Santa Monica. As they pass through Beverly Hills, she finally speaks.

"It was a Charlie Chan movie."

"What's that, sweetheart?"

"The script I was reading with Danny. It was a Charlie Chan movie. He has a part in it."

She's silent again until they pull up to the address. The street is long and wide, with palm trees lining the sidewalks. The houses are all large craftsman structures, with shallow front lawns and small driveways that lead to detached garages. Violet's house is painted white. The roof slopes down in front, creating a covered porch. A green Westport chair sits beside the front door, a wooden screen door slightly ajar.

As Hollis pulls into the driveway, Katherine asks, "Who lives here?"

"It belongs to a friend of your mother's. She's away and we thought it'd be better if you stayed here for a while."

"But why couldn't I have just stayed where I was?"

He parks the car, turns off the engine, and waves toward the home.

"Why would you want to stay in that small apartment when you could have this whole house to yourself?"

Hollis gets out and retrieves Katherine's suitcase from the back seat. He's crossing the lawn, halfway to the front door, when he realizes Katherine's still in the car. He walks back to the Buick.

"Darling, please."

Katherine has her arms crossed and chin pushed into her chest. He notices she's wearing her new dress, the one with the yellow flowers. She finally looks up.

"Is all of this because of Danny? I swear, Papa, we were only rehearsing."

Hollis stays with Katherine until Evelyn arrives with lunch. While they're eating, Kahn pulls up with his cousin's truck. Katherine's trunk and her remaining luggage are in the back for the second time in a week. Later, when Evelyn begins to help Katherine put some clothes away in one of the guest bedrooms upstairs, Hollis tells them he's going to the office.

Stopped behind a light at San Vincente, Hollis decides instead to head toward the coast. He figures someone at his mother's rest home will have shown her a copy of the *Post-Record*.

The parking lot, as usual, is empty. At the front desk, the young brunette he saw last time does her best to stop from grinning when she sees him.

After he knocks and enters the small room, he finds his mother sitting in her usual spot. The newspaper, the one with the story about him, is folded on her bed. Registering his presence, she opens her eyes and says, "They were passing it around at breakfast."

He sits on the chair next to the bed.

"I'm sorry, Mama. She's not my mistress. Please believe me."

She turns to face him.

"I know that, Son. My eyes aren't so bad I couldn't tell who it was."

She'd met Katherine only once, during a vacation. She hadn't liked her.

"That wife of yours, Hollis. Why couldn't you have chosen better?"

When he reaches out to put his hands on hers, she pulls them away.

"You could have had children of your own," she continues, her voice rising, "instead of just pretending to be a parent to that abomination."

"That's quite enough, Mama. There's no need to be cruel."

"I don't mean to be." She sighs heavily. "I just wanted more for you. I wanted you to be happy, to have a family. You have such love in your heart, Hollis, and it's been wasted."

"I'm happy, Mama." He adds, even though he's not quite sure it's true, "I've been happy with Evelyn."

She ignores this.

"What if you'd had a boy, Hollis? You could have taken him to the tide pools the way your father took you. You could have shown him so much, instilled in him a love of science and nature. And now it's too late."

He leans forward and reaches again for her hands. This time, she doesn't pull away from his touch.

"It's not too late, Mama."

"Yes, it is, Hollis."

She closes her eyes and leans back.

"Yes, it is," she repeats.

He's still holding her hands when her eyes slowly close

and she falls asleep. After ten minutes, he gives a squeeze, pulls his hands gently away from hers, and stands up.

On his way out the door, he whispers, "Goodbye, Mama."

Getting into the Buick, he looks at his watch. It's almost five. The show at the Cocoanut Grove will be starting in a few hours. He takes Pacific Coast Highway to Wilshire and heads for the Ambassador Hotel. After parking, he finds the door marked ARTISTS' ENTRANCE. He tries the knob. It opens onto a long hallway of dressing rooms. As he walks, he sees an open door where an older man is slapping the cheeks of a younger man. The younger man is wearing a tuxedo.

"Bunny," the older man says, "snap out of it. You're going on in half an hour."

Hollis can smell whiskey as he passes.

At the end of the hallway, a sign on a door says ROYCE. He gives a light knock.

"What is it, Barney?" Sadie calls out from inside. "I thought I had more time."

Hollis opens the door and enters the small space. Sadie's wearing a pink robe and sitting at a makeup table. She's looking into a mirror that's edged with light bulbs.

Her hair is pinned back, and she's applying makeup. He closes the door quickly behind him.

"Why, Mr. Mulwray, I'm surprised to see you. News on the street is that you'd thrown me over."

"You saw the paper?"

She grunts.

"Didn't everybody? You're quite the celebrity."

He finds a folding chair in the corner and sits down. On the back of the door, three gowns hang from a brass hook.

"It's not true."

Still applying makeup to the same spot, she says, "Which part? Throwing me over or being a celebrity?"

"Neither, Sadie. It's not what it looks like."

She stops with the makeup and turns to face him.

"Then who's the dame?"

"My daughter. A stepdaughter, you might say." Hollis briefly takes off his glasses and rubs his eyes. "It's complicated."

"Family man, eh?"

When she goes back to applying the makeup, Hollis notices that she's only putting foundation in one spot. Near the bridge of her nose, there's a patch of purple she's trying to cover up.

"Sadie, you've been hit."

She pauses for a second, then returns to hiding the bruise.

"Frank's back."

"I know, I saw him. He followed me the other day."

She begins to break down in shallow sobs.

"I didn't want to tell him, Hollis. He showed up the day after you took me home. He knew I'd been with someone. He forced me to tell him who."

"And that's when he hit you?"

"No, he didn't seem to mind at first. But then he learned who you were." She looks up and finds Hollis's face in the mirror. "He knew you had money, and he thought me being with you was some sort of put-down on him. Like he wasn't good enough or something."

"But he's not good enough, is he, Sadie?"

She turns from the mirror to face him.

"No, he's not. I hate him. I think I've always hated him."

Hollis leans forward on the chair, close enough to smell her perfume. Lilacs.

"Then why don't you leave him?"

"Where would I go? I only just got this job, and they don't pay much. I can't swing rent all on my own."

In the hallway there's movement. Footsteps. After a knock on the door, a voice says, "Ten minutes, Ms. Royce."

Sadie sniffs and calls out, "Thanks, Barney."

As she returns to the mirror, to finish her makeup, Hollis slips a hand into his pocket. In addition to some loose change and a handkerchief, he feels the key to Katherine's apartment.

"I know a place, here in the city," he says. "It's in a nice building and I've already paid for six months. You could leave Frank. It's the perfect solution."

She turns again to face him.

"Really? You mean it?"

"Yes, I'll come for you tomorrow. Will Frank be gone at all during the day?"

"He mentioned something about Santa Anita. An old buddy phoned last night with a tip. Supposedly a sure thing."

"Good." Hollis stands up. "As soon as he leaves, pack your bags. I'll come to get you around lunch."

There's more noise in the hallway. Hollis hears instruments being tuned as the musicians make their way to the stage.

She rises to embrace him. He can feel the warmth of her body through the thin robe.

"Do you mean it? You'll help me? Protect me, even?"

"Yes, Sadie. Tomorrow, around one. I'll come and get you."

She pulls him in for a long kiss.

Another knock on the door. "Five minutes, Ms. Royce."

Ending the kiss she says, "My show's about to start."

She sits down and he opens the door, the last of the

musicians leaving their dressing rooms. He's about to close the door when she calls out, "Hollis, wait."

He turns back.

She blows him a kiss and says, "Until tomorrow, Mr. Mulwray."

"Until tomorrow, Sadie."

By the time Hollis wakes up, the bed is empty. Evelyn is gone. Looking at the clock, he sees it's almost ten. Sunshine streams through the windows. It's going to be a hot day. Yawning and stretching, he gets out of bed. After showering, shaving, and getting dressed, he meets Kahn at the bottom of the stairs.

"Where's Evelyn?"

"Mrs. Mulwray has gone riding."

Hollis just nods and heads to the veranda.

"I have to go into town," Kahn calls out. "I will take the servants. Need some things for the house."

"That's fine," Hollis calls back.

The young Mexican girl follows him out to the patio, carrying a silver tray containing newspapers, a decanter of coffee, and an assortment of pastries. Hollis sits down and tries to meet her gaze but, once again, she refuses.

Hollis points to the tray and says, with his best accent, *"Me gusta."*

He's almost startled when she quickly looks up. Her eyes are dark, like almonds. She speaks, quickly and with passion.

"Perdóneme, señor. Y que Dios le ayude."

Hollis stares back blankly. The older servant scampers onto the veranda to retrieve the younger one.

"What did she say?"

"She said we should be back by lunch."

The younger woman is dragged back into the house by the wrist. As he's pouring himself coffee, Hollis hears car doors open and close. A minute later, there's silence.

He's rarely alone in the house. Kahn or one of the servants is always hovering around, doing some sort of chore. Cooking, cleaning, ironing. Even outside there's usually activity from the gardener or the chauffeur, but this morning everyone seems to have disappeared.

Finishing his second cup of coffee, Hollis hears noises behind him. Footsteps. At first, he thinks it's Kahn or one of the servants. Maybe they forgot something and had to come back. Or maybe it's Evelyn returning from her ride.

"Mr. Mulwray, we meet again."

Hollis turns to see Noah Cross standing in the open French doors, leaning on his cane. Claude Mulvihill stands behind him.

"Noah, what are you doing here?"

"Thought you and I should have another chat."

Hollis gets up as Noah and Mulvihill slowly advance.

"We have nothing to talk about. Bagby and your cronies will undoubtedly pull enough strings to win approval of the dam. You'll win, don't worry."

"Yes, I always seem to. However, there's something else I now want."

"And what's that?"

"Katherine."

Before Hollis can say anything, Cross adds, "Let's discuss this away from my associate, shall we?"

As Cross and Hollis walk on the grass and down the cobblestone path to the edge of the pond, Claude remains standing at the edge of the veranda. Resting the cane against his hip, Noah retrieves a pair of gold bifocals from his suit jacket. After putting on the glasses, he pulls out a checkbook and a pen.

"How much do you want?"

"For what?"

"For you to tell me where you're hiding her. I checked at the apartment building that was mentioned in the newspaper. She's gone, cleared out. I had the manager let me in."

"And how did you get him to do that?"

Noah waves the checkbook.

"Everyone can be bought. Name your price."

"You're crazy, Noah, if you think I'd tell you."

"Don't be a fool. Tell me where she is, and I'll give you as much as you want."

Hollis's face turns red with anger. He moves to slap the checkbook out of Noah's hand, but he's standing too close and instead he hits Noah hard across the face. The gold glasses go flying into the water.

"Claude!" Noah calls out.

Mulvihill lurches out from the shade of the patio and

approaches the two men. Cross turns without a word and begins to walk back toward the house, the cane creating holes in the grass with each step. Passing by Mulvihill, he says quietly, "You know what to do."

Before Hollis can make a move, Claude lands two quick punches to the gut. With the wind knocked out of him, Hollis drops to the ground, gasping for breath. As he tries to get up, Claude kicks him hard again in the stomach. The force sends him backward into the pond.

Hollis is disoriented by the sudden coldness of the salt water. Trying to escape, he frantically reaches out for rocks or air. But Claude's powerful hands keep him under the surface. The man is now also in the pond, the water up to Mulvihill's waist as he continues to keep Hollis submerged. Hollis fights to get free, to wrench Mulvihill's hands away from his body, but the larger man is just too strong.

Under the water, Hollis opens his eyes. He sees floating fronds, moss-covered stones, a red starfish perched on a white rock. He thinks back to his childhood room in Monterey. The drawings tacked to the wall. He recalls the facts he learned as a boy. A starfish has no brain and no blood. Hollis remembers the hours he spent with his father on the beach, peering into tide pools and gazing with wonder at the mysteries of life they would find there.

His vision becomes darker and darker as his final breath leaves his body in the form of bubbles that rise to the surface. The last thing Hollis sees is the starfish. No brain and no blood. Only water.

www.ingramcontent.com/pod-product-compliance
Lightning Source LLC
LaVergne TN
LVHW041629060526
838200LV00040B/1501